GW00374622

A new year dawned and I suddenly determined to challenge myself with shortage of time. In brief, I would write a short short story every day in succession. This little book contains some of the results.

To be honest (generally a foolish thing for a writer to be) a short written on a Monday requires a Tuesday as well. On Tuesday, you edit, you correct, you knock out ungainly sentences, you amplify . . . for you may suddenly discover a new meaning that had never occurred to you on the Monday. So you in effect rewrite. That's what Tuesdays are for . . . the writing of tiny masterpieces.

Most of these stories are fairly dark, glowing with gloom. I like it that way.

The Invention of Happiness

The Invention of Happiness

BRIAN W. ALDISS

THE INVENTION OF HAPPINESS
Copyright © 2013 Brian W. Aldiss

COVER ART
Copyright © Alison Soskice 2013

INTERIOR ART
Copyright © Brian W. Aldiss 2013

Published in October 2013 by PS Publishing Ltd. by arrangement with the author. All rights reserved by the author. The right of Brian W. Aldiss to be identified as the Author of this Work has been asserted by him in accordance with the Copyright, Designs and Patents Act 1988.

FIRST EDITION

ISBNs
978-1-848636-72-9
978-1-848636-72-6 (signed edition)

This book is a work of Fiction. Names, characters, places and incidents either are products of the authors' imaginations or are used fictitiously. Any resemblance to actual events or locales or persons, living or dead, is entirely coincidental.

Design & Layout by Michael Smith

Printed in England by the T.J. International

PS PUBLISHING LTD
Grosvenor House
1 New Road, Hornsea
East Yorkshire, HU18 1PG
England

e-mail: editor@pspublishing.co.uk
website: www.pspublishing.co.uk

Contents

PREFACE

Should an author concern himself about who his readers are? Should he worry about what they think of his writings?

Is not the world full of better and more cogent concerns?

These questions I raise without, hardly surprisingly, being able to answer them.

I raise them because I have been so entirely a writer all my long life, forever concerned with what to say and why I choose—or why I have been chosen—to say it.

Hardly a year has passed without the publication of a slender book of verse, a translation of the poems of Makhtumkuli, a novel, SF, a travel book, a selection of short stories, or a volume of social commentary.

The possible length of a tale has long been an interest. A case of curiosity.

One of my inventions was the Mini-saga. My Mini-saga project was to contain a story within fifty words. (Titles did not count within the bastions of that punitive fifty.) The *Daily Telegraph* embraced my idea, and we ran mini-story competitions for six successive years.

My determination from the start was that A Mini-saga should not be trivial; its spatial limitation drained narrative from the form; a moral aspect would remain.

Here is the example I offered my newspaper readers:

HAPPINESS AND SUFFERING

The doors of the amber palace
closed behind the young king.
For twenty years he dallied with

his favourite courtesan. Outside,
the land fell into decay. Warlords
terrorised the population.
Famine and pestilence struck,
of which chronicles still tell.
The king emerged at last.
He had no history to relate.

Some years after this was published, I discovered that a beautiful and cultured lady of my acquaintance carried about a cutting of this Mini-saga in her purse. What is more enthralling than fame?

Why, secrecy.

There is a destiny that shapes our ends, review them as we may.

When I phoned the *Telegraph* with my suggestion, I was working at the other end of the narrative scale, on a long trilogy concerning a planet called Helliconia.

And now? A new year dawned and I suddenly determined to challenge myself with shortage of time. In brief, I would write a short short story every day in succession. This little book contains some of the results.

To be honest (generally a foolish thing for a writer to be) a short written on a Monday requires a Tuesday as well. On Tuesday, you edit, you correct, you knock out ungainly sentences, you amplify . . . for you may suddenly discover a new meaning that had never occurred to you on the Monday. So you in effect rewrite. That's what Tuesdays are for . . . the writing of tiny masterpieces.

Most of these stories are fairly dark, glowing with gloom. I like it that way.

—*Brian W. Aldiss*

The Invention of Happiness

Wendy Aldiss, my darling daughter, whose dainty fingerprints are on this book.

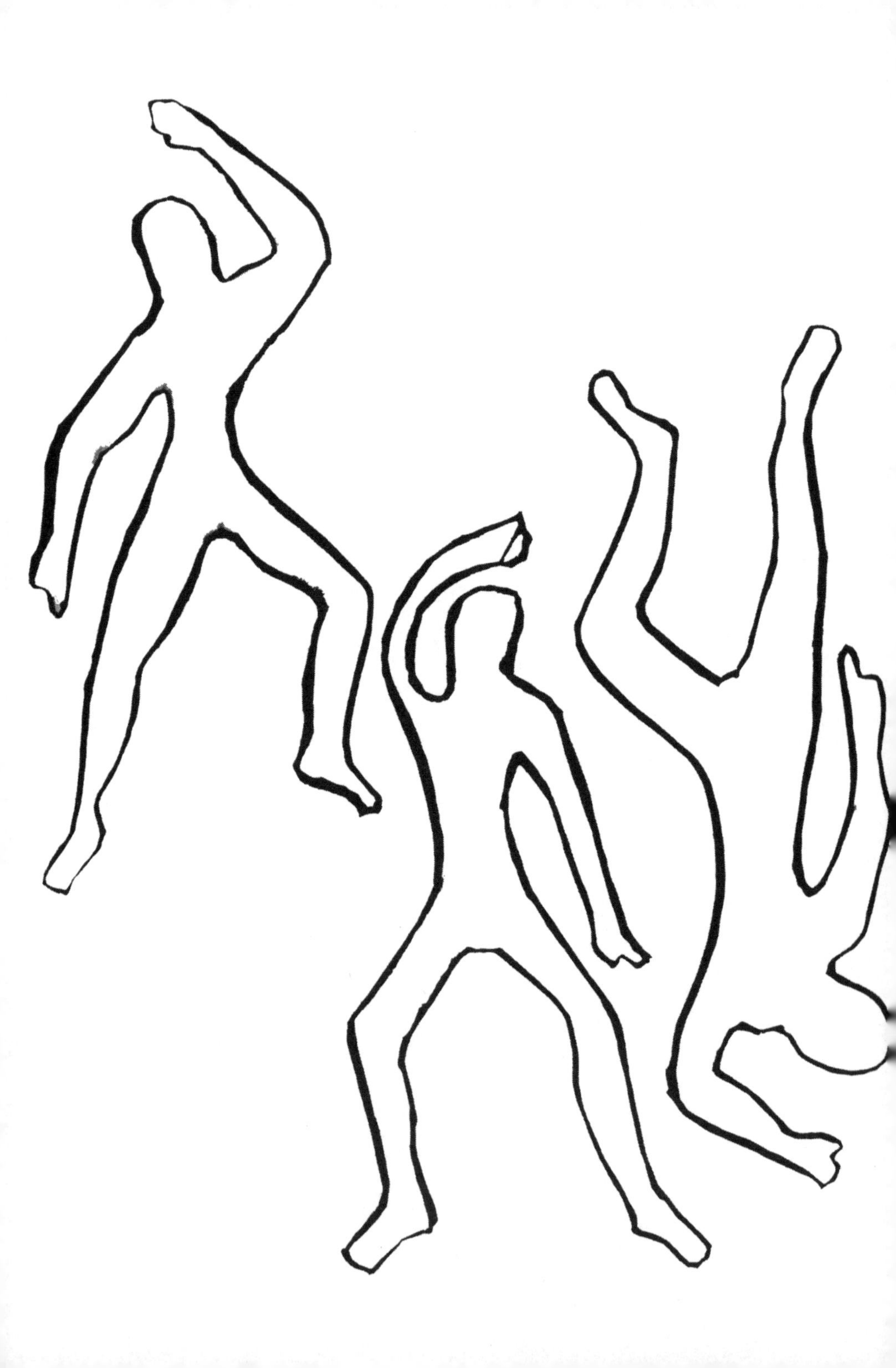

The Invention of Happiness

Those were happy days, when I was first married to my Chinese wife, Chi-Huru Li. Li was a psycho-analyst at the University of Liverpool, author of 'The Meaning Behind Beijing Opera', and of 'The Pleasures and Agonies of Human Kind'.

While I doted on this elegant lady, I also liked to engage her in disputes about the failings of humanity in general, a subject which, after all, afforded her much of her study material.

There was an occasion when Li and I had visited Stratford-upon-Avon to witness a performance of what in its essence was an ancient Chinese—should I call it a play or a charade? This fine charade centred upon the difficulties of sons and mothers and the suppressions enforced by those in power. The earliest surviving source for this play was something like thirty centuries ago, in the Zhou Dynasty.

Although staves as weapons of punishment have long since gone out of fashion, today's industrialised world has found adequate substitutes; while the human miseries of the drama remain with us still. Li and I agreed that, even allowing for the advances in medicine and science in our world today, the behaviour of mankind had not much improved over that span of time.

We enjoyed a meal in the theatre restaurant after the show, exchanged a few words with fellow diners, and drove home.

A week later, Li wrote to me from Liverpool. Here I copy what my darling writer said:

"I have discussed with my fellows," (she said) "and we have studied this question regarding human happiness, our hopes for the happiness of ourselves and others, and also the brevity of happiness when it descends on one or other of us. Mostly, we agree that happiness is a state of lesser duration than grief.

"When having to air such commonplace sentiments before our Principal, Lloyd Derekson, he drew our attention to an acute statement, made by the Venerable Bede long ago, in the 7th Century A.D.

"You probably know all this, but I can't resist quoting it.

"So picture an old man in a Northumbrian monastery, long ago in that dark century, a man we remember as the Venerable Bede. Picture the winter's night, a draughty hall, reed lights flickering, the good old fellow wrapped up against the chill.

"And this is what he said:

"'O King, It seems to me the present life of men on earth, in comparison with that time which to us is uncertain, as if when on a winter's night you sit feasting with your earldormen and brumali, and a simple sparrow should fly into the hall, and coming in at one door, instantly fly out through another. In that time in which it is indoors it is indeed not touched by the fury of the winter; but yet, this smallest piece of calmness being passed almost in a flash, from winter going into winter again, it is lost to our eyes. Somewhat like this appears the life of man, but of what follows or what went before, we are utterly ignorant'."

"Is happiness so brief? Aristotle held happiness, to be an ultimate aim of human life. He does not tell us how it can be achieved. Aristotelians and Epicureans both value happiness above all else, while differing in what they believe happiness to be. Aristotle thought virtue was necessary for one to be able to be happy. Whereas for Epicurus happiness was no more than rational hedonism.

"So we don't get very far. And then in the nineteenth century, Schopenhauer, the German philosopher, established a system of metaphysical pessimism. He saw the world as a 'vale of tears, full of suffering. All happiness is an illusion. Life oscillates like a pendulum, back and forth between pain and boredom'.

"He saw everyone's life history as a story of suffering, a continuing series of large and small accidents. Dr Samuel Johnson might agree with all that. Schopenhauer found inspiration in Buddhism, teaching pessimism as a way to happiness . . .

"Then there's Jeremy Bentham with his social reforms—but why go on?

7 The Invention of Happiness

All who examine this elusive quality of happiness seem to have no prescription for personal happiness. They're a doleful lot! We asked ourselves who, among the great men of the past, had taken any effective step to improve an individual's lot. What great invention could one say has been visited upon our poor beleaguered human race for its greater contentment? Must we just accept that brilliant dictum of the Bede's?

"Well, my treasured husband, here comes my answer.

"Let us suppose we have moved back in time. We arrive in the distant pasture and past of the Ming Dynasty, which was sustained for about three hundred years.

"We know that Chinese families often kept a trade, handed down from generation to generation.

"Here is a young man called Chai, who belongs to a family of house decorators. He has at this juncture put away his distemper brush to venture to a meeting with a young woman.

"It is a fine day, with a sky like blue porcelain.

"Chai lives in the city of Nanchang, where citizens' activities are strictly controlled; the result is a peaceful and prosperous century, although it must be said that Chai's family for several generations have often gone hungry. It is the unremarked custom of this great country.

"Certainly Chai has his anxieties—but nothing unaccustomed. He walks down a dusty street and enters a pleasant courtyard. Part of this courtyard is fenced about by judiciously planted clumps of acer trees.

"The young man meets a lady friend of his, by name Xaiy. They bow in greeting to each other. He touches her hand. She smiles and they wander together among the trees. Towards the back of the courtyard, the pair come unexpectedly on a large fat middle-aged man, greasy with cookery. Large pink shrimps and prawns hang on a line beside him.

"This unusual fellow has set up a table with a few chairs, in front of him; he is cooking some dishes. Various pots sizzle and steam beside him. Some containing meat, some containing parts of octopus, some containing vegetables, some a little of each. To one side, a large pitcher containing wine stands on the paving slabs.

The fat cook smiles at the young pair.

"'You would like a little snack, by the look of you,' he says in best Mandarin, gesturing. 'Please take a seat!'

"The young man and his lady are astonished to see this arrangement. They interrogate the man behind the table, who smiles and explains he had lost his job, his family have moved away to a sea port, and he wondered what to do next to earn a legal coin or two.

"He observed that there were people not willing or able to eat in their own homes. He had a bright idea. Perhaps he could arrange a little place, as in this Nanchang courtyard, to which people could come and—for a small fee—be fed.

"This, he said, was not as yet illegal. He smiled.

"But customers could be not only fed . . .

"People, he hoped smilingly, and his plump cheeks wobbled at the thought, would come to sit and eat something, and converse with each other, with friends or possibly with amiable strangers—strangers whom they met here at his table under the sweet acers. And all would be serene. His role was to smile, as now he did, and provide a little tasty snack and wine for his (here he gave an even wider smile) guests.

"Young Chai and his lady friend were enchanted. They ordered a little plate of spicy chicken chow mein, which they shared between them, held each others hands, laughed and chatted. And the sun shone on them.

"And other folk arrived, and were also charmed.

"With this anecdote, my treasured love, I present the story of the invention of the First Restaurant in the World. I hope to convince you to believe—as I do—that the greatest, most enduring step towards human happiness is—and has long been—the Restaurant. The Restaurant which has spread from that quiet Ming courtyard around the world." So the lady claims.

"In various guises, the restaurant has provided the one enduring benefit with which to solace the challenges and trials with which humanity otherwise aggravates itself."

These days whenever Li and I slip into the nearest café for a bite to eat, accompanied by a glass of wine, I think again of that genial cook and his table in the Ming Dynasty courtyard.

Who would have guessed how widely, how rapidly, his invention would spread?

And I believe that genial cook to be the greatest benefactor ever of the human race.

Beyond Plato's Cave

"I would like you to imagine," the technician said, "a family for whom television is entirely everything.

"There is a father and mother together with two sons and two daughters. They are all seated comfortably, looking towards the television screen. Indeed," said the technician, smiling, "they cannot look away, for their heads are secured from behind: well secured, so that they cannot even see one another. All any one of them can see is the activity showing on their big TV . . .

"Most of such activities are set in cities or the countryside. In the cities are cars, buildings, hospitals, prisons, and homes; while in the countryside there are woods, wide spaces, and numerous animals of various kinds, from lions and rhinos to cats, dogs, and fleas.

"Do you understand this situation?" the technician asked his audience.

"Yes," said the crowd of undergraduates in the audience, "although we do not yet see what moral you are going to draw from this unlikely situation."

"Moreover," said one female undergraduate, "we know you are simply giving us a modernised version of Plato's underground cave with the confined figures, which Plato describes in—book seven, I think it is, of his 'Republic'. What is your objective in doing this?"

To which the technician replied, "Well, Plato's cave is rather old hat, but the question he raises is still of great pertinence.

"You may recall that the conclusion is that an art exists which will enable us to see straight and to heal us from engaging in what is untruthful."

At this point one or two people were sneaking out of the lecture room.

It was nearing nine o'clock, when Episode Two was to be showing of the new series of *Doctor Who*.

Taking no notice of these deserters, the technician said, "We live by assumptions. For instance, we assumed with pride and delight that we could visit the Moon. NASA had landed Neil Armstrong there. But few people have been there since Armstrong. It's not only that the Moon is some distance away—it's too expensive to get there.

"And if you were there . . . Well, you can be photographed there, of course, but there's nothing else you can do. As for getting to Mars—which might prove more interesting—well, the same factors ruin any assumptions we may have. It's too far away, and too expensive."

He contemplated his audience, as they did him.

"So then, back to this sad imprisoned family, the hypothetical six who watch TV for all their lives."

"Lucky devils! Better than work," said a man in the audience and there was some laughter.

The technician ignored it. "The truth is that we have become enslaved by what television does. We think we know a great deal more than our predecessors. Certainly we know more about the fauna of Africa or Madagascar, or about what leading politicians are saying inside 10 Downing Street or the White House or in Berlin. But we have lost a sense of our selves in the universe—and yes, I do here include a religious sense of enquiry."

A hand shot up in the second row of the audience.

"You're generalising, though. I'm only an estate agent, but I can't help wondering, are we terrestrial humans the only intelligent species in the galaxy, or are there loads more like us? I mean, isn't that religious?"

The technician agreed. "Oh, we can ask the question. And unfortunately whatever conclusion we might come to, it would just be an assumption . . . "

So the discussion continued . . .

Old Mother

Old Mother lived alone, as she had done for centuries, in her hovel on the crest of one of the ridges on North Barrows, in a country much like this country.

She never went out. She looked out. Sometimes she saw Old Whatsit pushing along in a furrow, with a spade over his shoulder and a big white dog following him. Old Whatsit was a friend of Old Mother's. Oft times he left a parsnip and a spud on her step. They never spoke.

She moved slowly, creaking as she went. Two things she enjoyed: one was liking, the other was tapestry. As for tapestry, she sometimes did a stitch or two. As for liking, she liked herself and she liked her own smell.

What she did not like included other people and the Queen in her palace. She did not greatly care for the idea of Death, which disarranged things. But one night, lying on the floor under her rug, life fled from her.

She never moved again and a parsnip and a potato rotted out on her step.

Sharmish had been a daughter of Old Mother. Old Mother had kicked her daughter out at the time of the Two Worshipful Wars. She had then forgotten about her.

No longer was Sharmish particularly young, but she dyed her long hair yellow, padded out her bosom and wore the long purple garb, which was the style of the day. Her husband, about his duties, brought her to an inn on the Barrows, where they had quarrelled.

So Sharmish went walking, her pet parrot, Garo, on her shoulder. Spying a lonely shack perched on a high barrow, she had a possible vague, vile memory of an old woman who had thrown her to the four winds long ago. Going to the door, she kicked it open and marched in.

There lay Old Mother, motionless, face a gruesome grey. The entry of Sharmish had alarmed a Barrow Biter. The snake sought concealment. Shelter lay through the half-open mouth of the corpse, down its throat and into the desiccations of the belly.

Displeased, the daughter looked about her. Scarred by the ages, a table and chair maintained a weary presence. A wooden thing stood against a wall. A thin rectangular box stood in one corner, a long-handled axe in another. A pail half-full of dung, now humped and hairy, stood on a crude hearth, where sticks had long ago burnt to ashes. The woman, expressionless, stared at these dismal surroundings.

The Biter, supposing itself safe by now, popped its head out of the mouth of the corpse.

With one malicious movement, Sharmish seized up the axe, swung it, and severed the snake's head from its body. The blow sufficed to sever as well the head of Old Mother's corpse from its body.

Taking up the rectangular box, Sharmish set it on the table and opened up its lid.

Within the box lay fine silken tapestries, some gliding out on to the boards of the floor.

Here was a sea being portrayed, with big graceful fish swimming about a mermaid. A fishing boat sank on the horizon. Elsewhere, on another silken surface, creatures of the air were in flight, plunging or hovering about a kiddy's kite. Clouds ran through the portrayal, as waves had done in the first one. There were other beauties in the box. Sharmish did not study them, beyond reckoning that the collection would be worth a considerable amount of money.

She bundled the tapestries into a roll and rose to her feet. Kicking aside the head of Old Mother, she left the shack.

Not displeased, she made her way back to the inn.

There she would make peace with her husband. Or not, as the case might be.

Belief

One of the great Osbert Miller's sayings is treasured from his early childhood.

He was visiting his grandmother, Mrs. Aldridge, who brought out caskets of her jewellery to delight the boy. Indeed he was delighted. After turning various treasures about, Osbert said, "Grannie. I don't wish to be morbid, but when you're dead, can I have them?"

Osbert Miller (later known as Oz the Believer) grew up to be one of the great names in electronics in the 1970s. He established himself in what became BBC TV, moving after two years to Hollywood, where he developed the electronics department within MGM. Always successful, always glum.

He met Jo Clim at MGM. Clim, a defrocked priest, had no knowledge of how he reached New York. He lived in Arkansas. No doubt drink and drugs had something to do with his change of scene.

Clim and wife shacked up with Miller on the wealthier side of Brooklyn. There he preached, on the sidewalk, his theory of Belief and its virtues. The wife danced. Miller listened.

"Mary Magdalene was pregnant when she arrived in Bethlehem," said Clim. "She was a smart woman. She went to the hotel Reception to claim the room she believed Joseph had booked—only to find that the old fool had forgotten to book as planned.

"The hotelier was apologetic but his hotel was crowded; the best he could do for Mary was to install her in his shed, where he sheltered cattle. Mary was furious with Joseph, and made the old sod sleep outside in the cold. Just deserts . . .

"Mary's kid, Jesus, was nothing much, but she spoilt him. As a young guy, with his gang, Jeez almost ruined the temple and later was very rude to Pontius Pilate. He was due to be hanged, but he got away and another member of the gang, Jude, was hanged in his stead.

"Jeez never said anything clever," Clim's tale continued. "Most of what we read in the Gospels—the miracle of the loaves and fishes, for example—was made up later by the cleric we know as Mark."

"So what's your point?" Miller asked, as they sat together drinking the little wife's coffee.

Clim wagged a finger. "Believe in Belief. The Gospels, the whole story of Jesus Son of God, may be absolute twaddle, but we should believe in it. Belief's beneficial! Isn't the Bible's tale a better story than the true business of the young hoodlum. Belief . . . Those who find nothing to believe in, true or false, are lost . . . "

Miller, between times, thought deeply about Belief. "What about Evolution?" he asked Clim, one day.

Clim's wife replied, ticking off sentences with a slender finger. Luckily, she was as deluded as was Clim.

"Ah, that theory is a grand structure for belief. A few birds—finches or whatever—inhabit various islands. So what? We are descended from some kind of ape? What? Sure it happens just that we look more like apes than like horses. But there's been no progression! It's just that progression suits us, nowadays, so we believe in it. We came across things we could eat, that's all. But it suits us to think this is progress. Not progress or science." She smiled. "It's just good old Belief."

Miller saw that all such arguments could be better expressed. He went about preaching. Everyone liked Belief. The proletariat who watched football matches, a worthless, crude sport, could believe themselves to have importance. Some folk tried Belief in themselves.

Grannie's family jewels—which finally went to Miller's sister—were valueless unless various experts declared them valuable. Rembrandt's daubs, how happy we were to believe them masterpieces. How happy folk were to believe the Belief Guru's version of wisdom . . .

After The Party

It was totally dark. It seemed to be totally dark. His name was Keith. Yes, Keith Sutton. It was Sutton? Sudden? Sudden hero of Garambia . . .

And he was er live. Live.

Could he be under a car? Something heavy lay over him. Not a car. He was not crushed. A car—what was it? Door. A car door . . . He didn't think his body was broken. He could not feel his legs. He tried to reach for them. Black sight. African? Afri can't . . . He became stupefied again, as if drifting on a breeze.

He was cold. He roused. Part hot. His vision was blurred, but day was now light. He could see grass and weed patches, and stones, without moving his head. Couldn't move his head.

This limited outlook was just a smear across his vision. He stared at it vaguely, admiring grarz. Graz was green. He marvelled that grass was green. Had anyone planted this patch of grass? Had it arrivedere on its own—so that he could see it?

This limited viewpoint must be important becoz it had been arranged. Ranged so that he could study it. Had it always been there? Had he? Imagine he was in pain . . .

A white thing lay on the tufts of grass. He had not noticed it previously. His eyes hurt when he strove to focus on it. He fancied it was shaped like a Gambnuh, a hand. A moment past when he failed to be a-where? of anything. Staring again, he muttered, "So like a hand . . . " Perhaps it was a hand. A female, a woman's hand.

It was not his hand. He thought no more about it. He heard groaning. Lissening, he believed it must be his own groaning. His mouth was—yes, there it was, a thing erpart. It seemed to drip. That was not pleasant. Oh, but being unpleasant . . . suddenly he thought, "I've bin in a car crash . . . "

So then he felt fairlicertain that he had been in a car crash. Not a pleasant thing to happen. Had it happened? Had he been driving? Was he under part of the car now? Conviction grew that that was so. He was under part of the car and he had been driving. He found he was shaking with fear—just a little shake. A little fear. Fear he'd felt erbroad . . . where wozzit?

Under. Yes.

Bushmead. Bushmead, village near Bedford. He lived in Bushmead. Had he been turning off the main road? That long laaane.

So no one had found him yet. He could die here. Could it be he was dead already? Was this like what it was like to be dead? The stillness, the green of the grass, the weight on his body, very likely a gravestone.

Oh, and that hand, pale hand. Suddenly he remembered Rosie. Had Rosie—yes, Rosie had been, been in the car with him.

He fought to see beyond that hand, up the elbow to the shoulder, the body. Was Rosie dead too? He could not move. His efforts to move had made his legurt. He worked one of his aaarms free, free enough to feel down that trapped leg. The hand returned—caymup—till he could just sort of see its finger-tips. Ssshhtained with blood.

He didn't care. The leg was none of his business. And now his brain pulsed until he remembered something else. Funny how such tatters remained. The party. The binge. His cousin's birthday. In Birmingham it was. Old chums. Ah, the Gambia. Singing!

He closed his eyes in pain. "Don't wanter know. Just lie here." But cousin George, if he was Keef Stutter, then he had got hold of . . .

He tried to look at the grass and the stones, but something in him knew bitter and admitted that he had fallen for old George's girl, Ruby. Or was it Rosie?

He had got her in the car and drove off with her. Of course they'd had a fair old bit to drink. It was only a bit ovver laugh.

She had shrieked and she had laughed. It was Ruby, wasn't it?

And once he'd gotter to Bushmead . . . "Ruby!" he called. Too feeble, throat so full of phlegm. "Ruby! Ruby, pet!"

He strained to look again at the hand lying on the grass. Rosie . . . It was still there. The grass was still there. Colourless.

As far as he could tell . . . no, better not think that. Still he was angry with her. "Rosie, you bitch, don't die, you hear?"

He thought he heard a faint whisper answering, but a breeze was getting up. Stupid. Chill . . . Not like in Africa.

If it rained, he would get wet. Why not? He thought. There was this thing, this door, was it? Over him. But was someone there? "Wanna cupper tea," he muttered.

He checked the patch of grass. Funny. It was not green, as he had imagined. It was blood red. He'd have fun, telling . . .

Hell, he'd been driving in the Gambia to urn money for deprived kids. Months agog, a year agog, was it? Oh hell and shit, really . . .

Old mates. . . . . Still he lay there.

Our Moment of Appearance

Imagine that you are sitting in a row close to the stage. Our theatre is immense and largely filled. A silence falls on the audience; they are aware that the play is about to begin, to unfold a cornucopia of events.

The stage itself is neutrally lit, as yet empty and expansive. A door rear left opens, with light shining forth from an imagined room we shall never see; we have to believe it exists, as we wait in our seats in silence—those of us who do not act.

But we are not concerned with the imaginary room. Our attention is fixed on the actor who has emerged from it and now comes forward towards the footlights.

Or take another moment, a similar moment, almost the identical moment. Here the actor—that same actor—waits in semi-darkness behind the door, unseen by the waiting audience. His moment comes. He pushes open the door and steps briskly forward across the stage towards the lights, the audience.

Some of us sitting there will be aware of this moment with its two alternatives.

We might say that the moment works almost psycho-analytically, forms an unrecognised analogue of that time when, as a babe new born, we see to our astonishment the living world beyond the womb, the living world through which—though this perception is unlikely to dawn as we cry for the mighty breast hanging over us—we will play out our living roles.

To the actor opening an artificial version of our lives, his appearance on stage carries a graver implication. The compulsion is on him to speak. I may address the audience directly. For I was an actor, and experienced that immense, intense, moment before silence is broken. Here the actor experiences a suffocating, surrogating, experience of love and fear.

He must cut that knot with speech.

Possibly he says, "Now is the winter of our discontent made glorious summer by this son of York."

He may have a considerable part in the play we are here to watch, or he may simply be a kind of herald, not at all central, but rather an announcer of sorts, with a scant half-dozen lines to his role. We may never see him again, this herald who comes from the unknown towards the footlights.

His hope may be that this role will lead him to greater roles, on the stage or possibly in film. But that is hardly his concern at this particular moment, nor is it likely to be ours, the attendant audience.

It might be that we are related to this actor, his father, his mother, his brother, or aunt. In which case, we nudge each other with an excitement apart from the anticipated drama of the play. Perhaps we even catch the eye of the actor advancing across the stage.

But that momentary distraction is brushed aside. I, as the actor involved, have no time for metaphysical speculations. My role is me. I am the role.

So great, so metaphysical, is this that I take . . . . . . I take one of my prancing steps too far forward, and fall off the stage into what is appropriately called the Pit.

I fall on the piccolo player—a man I never liked. This accident breaks his neck. He dies instantly. His name was Ralf Schuster.

As for me, I lie there in agony, in despair, having shattered both my acting career and my right leg.

A stretcher is found for me. As I am being carried prone from the auditorium and theatre to an ambulance, I hear the coarse laughter of the audience.

Proles! Scum! Fascists! Who would wish to entertain such a mob? Not I! Never again . . .

The Bone Show

In the world-wide struggle of the Second World War, the tide was slowly turning against Nazi Germany.

Tommy Keen had volunteered to join the British Army at the age of seventeen. He was now with a detachment of the Mendips, pressing into Westphalia towards the town of Bielstadt.

The detachment entered a village ruined by bombs and gunfire. Dead bodies lay rotting in the streets.

Sergeant Thorpe kicked open the door of a detached house and they burst in. The rooms were empty—except for a kitchen. Here, wedged behind a table lay a body in civilian clothes.

"Search him, Keen," Thorpe ordered. "He might have a bit of cash in his pockets."

As Tommy was shifting the table, the supposed dead body hefted itself up on one elbow and started firing at random with a service revolver. Sergeant Thorpe shot the man dead. Tommy Keen fell to the floor in agony. He had been shot in the foot.

"Get up, man," said Thorpe. "Time we was in Bielstadt."

When the war ended, Tom Keen got a job on one of the London newspapers, then situated in Fleet Street. He remained a trifle lame, but his wounded foot did not bother him greatly and he enjoyed his work as a sub-editor on 'The Striking Clock'.

Keen had married Rachel, a young woman of Jewish ancestry whose parents had died in Buchenwald. Rachel had been saved as a babe-in-arms by a kindly German couple who secretly deplored the Nazi regime. This couple, the Zommers, now aged, had moved to settle in England near the Keens.

When a new movie came along, heralded up and down the country as the latest and greatest Bone movie, starring a famous actor as the legendary spy, Tom and Rachel decided to take the Zommers with them to see the film, with a supper afterwards as a special treat. And Tom had been chosen, as a privilege, to review this marvellous film for 'The Clock'.

They arrived early at the cinema, to find a dense queue at its door. Everyone, it seemed, had an urgent need to see *Guns of Grosvenor*, with Witlock Waine in the lead role of Bone.

The Keen party managed to get four seats together near the screen. Following half-an-hour of adverts, the moment came when, over its typical trademark, O.R. Studios presented *Guns of Grosvenor*. Many in the audience began clapping.

Action began immediately, with a car chase through London's busy streets and a lightly dressed young woman driving a tractor—driving it faster than the cars and smashing them up. Our hero, Bone—M calls him Hamilton—rushed from a building and jumped onto the tractor. Cinema audience claps.

Soon he and the girl were invited to the Houses of Parliament, where they were begged to save Heathrow Airport from destruction at the hands of unknown enemies. The prime minister appeared, whereupon Bone uttered his famous saying, "My name is Bone, Ham Bone." Wild cheering in the auditorium.

From then on, cunning and violence increased. Hanging on externally to the tail of an airliner, Bone made it to Aleppo and a swanky cocktail party. The villain appeared, disguised as an Arab. There were dramatic scenes in the desert, followed by brutal action near an active volcano, where the villain assembled a small army. Then Orl Rite Studios got us onto the roof of a speeding train, where a fight was in progress. The girl won because the villain had his head removed by the arch of a low bridge. Cheers from the cheaper seats.

She made a joke about wanting to express her relief. This to Bone, who had been whizzing up and down in an elevator shaft, dodging bullets. Finally, the two warring sides were locked into an old manor house which Bone set on fire. He alone escaped. All the rest perished. As the movie ended, the audience cheered and clapped.

Later that night, Tom Keen sat in his office at 'The Clock'. He had written his review of the Bone film. Now as he read it through, he realised he had actually reviewed the film's audience. He knew that of course the majority of that audience had lived in times of peace; they had not known war. Yet there were all kinds of threats to peace, from Muslim malcontents if none others. There were various riots, with a few people hurt. This was a peaceful country, superficially at least. What was it that prompted O.R. Studios to make such senseless stuff? Well, money for one thing . . .

But what was it prompting people to applaud two hours of extreme violence? Did they unknowingly wish for another war?

He screwed up his review and began again.

The Great Plains

The house where the Kingstones lived, and had lived for almost twenty years, stood on a slight rise above the road to Tonbridge. Ray and Madge Kingstone had an adult daughter, Claudia, whose marriage had not worked out, and two shaggy old dogs which had been Airedales in their youth.

Ray Kingstone was mayor of Farcompton, five miles away. His big problem at the present was being forced by the difficult economic situation of the country to close down Farcompton swimming pool; the site would then be taken over by a milk depot, which—it was calculated—would bring more money into the urban coffers.

But on this summer's day, Ray and Madge were preoccupied with the arrival of their son Roger, recently returned from a site on the Dnieper river. As Claudia's marriage had failed, so Roger's ambition to be a poet had failed. However, he had landed a job with a film unit. This occupation had taken him out to film for the BBC on the battlegrounds and desolate eastern reaches of Belarus.

Ray and Madge were in the garden when a limousine pulled up in the drive and Roger climbed out. He looked weary, but smiled as he shook hands with Ray and patted his back, and hugged and kissed his mother.

They urged Roger and his chauffeur indoors for a coffee.

"I actually can't stop at all," said Roger, looking wildly about. "I've got to be in Salford for a meeting by 1pm."

"We were longing to hear all about your trip," said Madge. "Can't we phone them?"

"No, we can't. There's too much at stake." He rose. His coffee cup was half-full. "I'll just use your loo. Then we must get on our way. Sorry and all that . . . "

Ray stood unhappily outside the lavatory door.

He heard his son say, "Well, go on, *pee* if you're going to," presumably addressing his own penis.

Roger reappeared. "Sorry, Dad. It was hell out there. The BBC want to scrap our excellent work! Might offend the Russians!"

As he grabbed the arm of the chauffeur, urging the man on, he thrust a folded sheet of paper into his father's hand.

"I wrote a poem. Old times' sake . . . Just three blunt and brutal rhymes . . . All for bloody Belarus. Love to Mum!"

Then he was gone. The car roared off down the road.

An Army Winters on the Great Plains

On this unending land lies long deep frost
Where I, once soldier, have been lost,
My unit strafed, all frozen rivers crossed,
All bridges broken. What riposte?
Although we were by icy furies tossed—
Gained we ten kilometres—at cruel cost!

Yes, yes, our generation, harshly bred,
Held little thought but Warfare in its head
Where there flamed Glory, so our Leader said—
Injury, hardship, how manlike you bled;
All this beneath our banners, never shed.
Alas, those flags now wrap the dead instead . . .

So look—this endless plain, where layers of cloud
And savage winds scream of our pain aloud,
We feed—it's done with shame, our heads are bowed—
On mortal heroes' flesh. Ah well, no prayer, no shroud!
We soldier on, un-dead, unknown, a crowd
Defeated. But we're told the Nation's proud!
Just as the Beloved Leader vowed.

—Roger Kingstone

CAFE GRINGO

What Befell the Tadpole

On a fine spring night, the moon was all but full. The countryside was hushed and a wind blew across Southern England.

That wind carried unusual micro-organisms, brought from a Kent laboratory. The micro-organisms, harmless enough, induced a temporary increased intelligence in all it met with.

Wolfgang was a mongrel dog of medium size. He had a rough white coat marked with two patches of black. Wolfgang was lying in his basket in the kitchen. His lead was still on, its handle tied to the oven door, preventing him from wandering about in the small hours.

He sat up, sniffing.

Quietly, methodically, he began to gnaw at his lead.

He had it in two in no time. He padded over to the door; it was locked and he could not open it.

Wolfgang scrambled up on to the window sill. The window was ajar, letting in the fresh night air. With a fore-paw, he pushed it wide open.

It was nothing for him to jump down into the garden, to cross the lawn, scale the wattle fence, and be away.

Soon he was down the street and into a field—and from the field was into open countryside.

He ran for the pleasure of it, front and rear legs almost meeting under his body and then immediately stretching away, as far as possible, fore and aft, before returning. He was aware only of movement, of freedom, as he rushed lightly, alight, across the untenanted turf.

Clairey Baker lay awake in the double bed, her husband, sleeping restlessly, lay close by her. It was too close. She pushed him away and then sat up.

A slender beam of moonlight cut between the two willow curtains.

Holding the palms of her hand against her eyes, she reflected on how stupid she was. Her job down at the employment office reminded her every day that she did not talk properly and had a whining accent. She had once been proud of it. She spent her evenings with an ice cream from the fridge, watching silly TV shows.

And then—Lorry beside her. Gormless. She had once thought him a comedian because he laughed at everything.

She and Lorry—it was Laurence, she remembered—had got together over drinks at a friend's one night. For Clairey it had been the height of romance, 'Romance'—how she had loved the word; so grown up! Now they still had a go, Saturday nights, but it was no fun any more. She did not like Saturday nights much.

Clairey climbed out of bed. Cautiously, quietly, she got dressed. Lorry slept on. She went downstairs. The third and fourth steps creaked loudly as usual.

She put on her shoes in the hall, unlocked the door, and went out into the fresh night air. She walked determinedly down the street towards the post-graduate school.

The River Deane ran smoothly between its banks. To one side was a small reedy pool, separated from the currents of the main stream. Here, water was calm. Here lived the tadpole. It was alone. One by one, its contemporaries had been swallowed up by a visiting perch.

The tadpole swam lazily among the reeds. It had suddenly realised there was a great future ahead of it—a transformation, and then an intense freedom of an entirely novel kind. She tried to visualise jumping . . .

These thoughts filled her with a kind of infant joy.

Suddenly the perch was back and the tadpole was gone. But there was always hope on such spring nights.

The Sand Castle

When I was appointed Chair of the Companion Guild, funded by Bournemouth Council, I gladly accepted the post. Christine Rivers was moving to that seaside resort. I could follow.

Of course, there was the sea. I had no great liking for the old town; but I intend this report to be more about Christine and her affairs than about me.

I observed that Christine's friends, who were many, always used her name unshortened, and never the more intimate 'Chris'.

Christine bought a fair-sized house up a side-street; from the windows on the upper story one could catch a glimpse of the sea. So into that upper story she placed beds for her two grandchildren, Flavia and Bernard.

Some years before this, Christine had been divorced from an eminent Right Wing politician (with whom she managed to remain on patchily good terms).

For a while she had lived with Mike, a minor official in the Save the Children organisation. Mike was often away in Africa. He turned and spurned Christine when she took on Flavia and Bernard, her daughter's children.

What of this dark daughter, by name Oriel—meaning 'golden'? She took up with Eddie Gissing, a descendant of a Victorian novelist. He worked in the BBC TV centre. They married. He was unfaithful, and she divorced him after five years, having born the two children.

I saw Oriel occasionally. For instance, once in the Ritz Hotel tea rooms, where Americans liked to meet.

Oriel was sitting over coffee cups with an older man, both deep in conversation. Oriel wore a smart black dress. I went over and said hello.

"Haven't seen you for a year or more." I said.

"This is Paul Sanderson," she said by way of response.

He looked coldly at me, while her regard was scarcely warmer. I felt I should ask her when she last saw her children, but their quiet hostility deterred me.

"You wanna join us?" Sanderson asked, in an unwelcoming tone. So he was American.

"I can see you're busy," I said, half-turning to go.

"Not at all," Oriel said. "We are simply relaxing. Not busy... Having a chat, as you might say."

So I left, wondering if this phrase, Having a chat, was to be regarded as laughable, as common...

Back in that old seaside resort, I saw Christine now and again. She was always cheerful or, to put it more accurately, always cool and collected. The children seemed happy in her care. She never scolded.

One Sunday, I took them all onto the beach, partly to meet my son Michael by my previous marriage. He was older than either Bernard or Flavia. We all went swimming. The sea was cold but we jollied each other along. Just as, in life, we jollied each other along.

Mike asked Flavia—to whom he had taken a fancy—

"Shall we build a huge sand castle?"

"Oh yes," she said, clapping her hands together. "I'm going to build a whopping great celebratory sand castle when Mummy comes back..."

I noted that Christine's back was turned, as she towelled and dried down Bernard's sandy little body. With all the noises surrounding us, of sea and sunbathers, she had not heard her grand-daughter's remark; nor had Flavia intended she should. She could reveal to someone apart from the broken family that she still longed for her mother, for the chilly Oriel.

And how, I asked myself, would this loss affect the adult Flavia? There are sorrows no Save the Children groups can eever entirely heal.

The Village of Stillthorpe

It seems I was sitting peacefully on a bench in the courtyard of a house, idly watching a waterfall. A fairly small waterfall, but the water had a drop of five or six feet.

Slowly I came to realise the water was continuously recycled and that somewhere out-of-sight there was a pump providing all the action.

Could it be, I wondered, that there was a similar motivation driving humanity on. While I indulged in this not particularly intelligent speculation, a friend of mine arrived and reported to me a story she had heard.

This is the story she told me. A man in middle age was sitting on a bench outside the hilltop village of Stillthorpe, enjoying the summer sun.

A fellow in a straw hat came along, doggedly making his way uphill. Seeing the occupant of the bench, he stopped. A sturdy fellow. He was poorly dressed and his boots were dusty and worn.

"Is that the village of Stillthorpe on the hill yonder?" he asked. Hearing that it was so, he asked what the people of the village were like."

The man on the bench asked him a question in return. "What were the people like in the village you have left?"

"Oh," said the other, "since you ask, they were real rogues, a whole lot of miserable thieving bastards. I wouldn't trust a one of them."

"Well," said our friend on the bench, "You'll find the folk in Stillthorpe are just the same."

The traveller drew himself up as if for battle.

"We'll soon see about that," he said and, scowling, he passed on up the hill.

The middle-aged man on the bench was just deciding he had been idle for long enough, and could do with a pasty and a pint of ale, when another man came along up the hill.

This newcomer on our scene wore a cap and was poorly dressed. He was a slender fellow. He stopped to greet the sitting man and ask if that would be the village of Stillthorpe he saw at the top of the hill.

He was told it was. He nodded and asked what sort of people lived in the village.

The man on the bench then asked the question he had put to the earlier passer-by. "What were the people like in the village you have left?"

The man in the cap sighed with regret, saying, "Since you ask, I must say I loved them all. They were charming—honest, hard-working, kind to the last man. And woman."

And the man on the bench said, "I think you'll find the folk in Stillthorpe are just the same."

My woman friend and I chuckled over the neatness of this story, and over its morality.

Only later did it occur to me to wonder what would happen if the second man in the cap met the first man in the hat in Stillthorpe high street.

Would they fight? Would the man in the hat shove the other man out of the way, or perhaps even punch him? Or would the man in the cap take the other to have a beer and, listening to his woes, try to calm him?

The tidiness of a moral tale has great appeal, rather like the confidence of the pump working my waterfall.

Alas, moral tales are one thing. Life is another.

We all have to live in our own Stillthorpes.

In one street, you proceed with caution.

In the next street, you find everything is fine.

You have made this village yourself.

We all have many streets to cross.

There's no real Stillthorpe at the top of our hills.

Of course, you could be lucky and come across the man sitting on that bench, fully prepared to respond to your idle questions . . .

Peace and War

"Come in, Pemberton," said Oliver Rawlings. He was sitting at his desk when Ron Pemberton entered the office. Rawlings did not invite Pemberton to sit down, as he usually did.

So Pemberton stood there, not speaking, while his boss talked about the continuing recession afflicting all of Britain, moving on from there to recite the company losses, until he came to the piece about being forced to part with valuable staff.

Ron Pemberton feared it was coming. Now it had come, all full of regret and polite commiseration. The farewell shake of the hand. Rawlings, it seemed, genuinely upset.

Pemberton, pulling on his mac and leaving the building, was also genuinely upset. Where, for Christ's sake, was he in his mid-fifties to find another job?

Back home—well, he'd have to sell up, for a start, and find—"oh, I don't know"—possibly a flat.

There was a note from Daisy. Daisy was the Iranian girl, sharp flashing smile with brilliant white teeth, dark liquid eyes, glorious streaming black hair—oh, what a honey, bright as a button! Her note said, 'I cleaned up. Cannot come next week. See you Thursday week. Love.'

Ever since Evelyn, 'the wife', had died, Ron's erotic fancies had centred round Daisy. Yet something no-nonsense about her had warned him not to touch. Iran—not a popular country in the national imagination, but oh, its young women . . . Why had Daisy left? He did not enquire. She did not tell.

That night, there was little sleep for Ron Pemberton. In one of those mysterious caesuras encircling three in the morning, he heaved himself out of bed. It was an early October night, not cold. He looked out of the window. He put on slippers, went downstairs, looked out of another window. There lay the little garden he had tended, the little garden he would have to leave.

Moonlight bathed the garden with silver, transforming it. Now it was an early painted masterpiece.

Its beauty cleared his mind of any other thought.

So beautiful . . . Unmoving. Transfixed.

He stood, taking in this unclouded soul of peace. A slight movement caught his eye. The cat from next door emerged from behind a bush, to make its way over a patch of silvered grass, into the clump of poppy. So it disappeared. Ron liked the cat and hoped it appreciated the sheer loveliness of its surroundings. He had planned to lure the cat into his house some day, to be stroked and petted.

But, of course, he would soon have to leave all this.

He turned from the window, sighing. He switched on the electric kettle to make himself a mug of tea.

Then he switched on the television, tucked into a corner, its aerial balanced on the disused bread bin.

The 4 a.m. BBC news was showing. The screen filled with hoards of men clutching staves. This was Iran, no less. Demonstrating against injustice. Then further Eastward. More injustice. Mobs in city centres. Fires blazing. Injuries. Further east still.

Now men on horseback in a central square. Massed crowds protest. A man, bloodily wounded, dragged off by a guy wearing an unstrapped helmet, strap dangling as he led his victim away to be shot. Tortured and shot.

Further east still. Women's bodies lying against a fence. A man madly shouting as a mass of leather-clads closed in on him. Some folks praying, others fighting.

Violent firing, fires, people running or screaming, further East. Blood. Now in Kyrgyzstan in Central Asia.

In all that great stretch of the world, no justice, no peace. Hell.

Ron switched off. He had his own worries.

The Vintage Cottage

A possible poem was buzzing in my head as I passed our local church. Church doors were open, bells were ringing. Young Laura Cleeve was coming towards me, pushing her bike.

"Looks as if there's going to be a wedding," I said.

"It's just the usual Sunday morning service, Jean," she said. She cast an odd look at me: fish thrown back into sea . . .

"Good god," I said, "I'm so absent-minded. So it's Sunday!"

"It happens to us all." she said. I thought I glimpsed a sneer behind her platitude. She pushed on without saying a word more. But, I told myself, I'm a painter. One of my still-lifes appeared in last month's 'RA Magazine'. Which Laura can't claim.

And I'm a poet. A poem due to be published shortly in a Salzberg magazine. Just to myself as I headed for Vintages, I quoted one verse I particularly liked of my recent poem :

"There stand the married couple, never apart
Though she has learnt what Togetherness means—
Her cooking and cleaning, her knickers, his jeans,
He'll show her his penis but never his heart . . . "

Yeah, that was it. The divorce, five years ago now, still feeling down about it. Jean Pottle, born in the back streets of Bognor, destined for better things. Driven by that big heavy mother of mine. She hated men. But then perhaps I do too.

I was nineteen when Dennis married me. He worked in the council offices and appeared to have prospects. A bit of a lad . . . Always cheerful. Always bloody cheerful . . .

And I had discovered that Pottle had once meant 'half a gallon'... Yeah, that was me, half a gallon. Never a full bottle.

Turning off the side street, I entered the small black door labelled VINTAGES. Beneath this, someone had written, The Old and Anguished Please Apply. I liked that.

Inside, Hettie Blanquette, pronounced Blanket, and Gloria were bright and cheerful, looking after everyone. They had three pokey little rooms, plus kitchen, leading one into another—the property had been a cottage for two centuries. Beyond, a little courtyard where nobody trod. Aged persons were sitting about, in one room watching television on a small screen.

I helped with the cleaning, with washing mainly hands and faces and with talking and listening to the aged tenants.

Most of them were concerned with how they could manage. or why they never saw X. They would say, "Maybe X is having a love affair," and laugh. Never that X might have died.

I talked with—or rather, listened to—a woman who had come originally from Lithuania. She had forgotten where it was.

"You'd best enjoy your old age," she said. "You only get the chance for it once." She knew this joke had amused me, so she repeated it, adding, "Trouble is, it's bad for your back . . . "

The intellectual in Vintages was Sydney C. Hull. Hull was eighty-nine, frail, but still eloquent. He knew I was a poet.

"Ah, here's our poetry friend!" he would say. "Come and talk to me." I would sit on the edge of his armchair and he would take my hand into his boney and fragile grasp.

Something he had read in 'The Times' had vexed him today.

"You see, my dear, they quote President Truman. For whom I have, believe me, great admiration. But they quote him as saying that the nuclear weapon the Americans dropped on Japan—thus ending that hideous conflict—as 'harnessing the basic power of the universe'. When anyone talks so grandly, we have good reason to fear, would you not say?"

"At least that nuclear strike marked a new epoch," I said.

"New epoch? Don't you start, love! New epochs bring. . . ." He broke into a short spasm of coughing. "What do they bring? What was I going to say? New epochs . . . well, new expectations."

"No more wars?", I suggested.

"Er, yes and no. I mean, apart from Europe and the U.S.A., and you might say China, might you . . . What was I going to say? Well, there are wars all over the globe, aren't there?"

"You're a poet. You know that if you're killed in a minor war it does greatly bugger up your life. 'Red lips are not so red as the stained stones kissed by the English dead...'"

The next day, Sidney held my hand. "What I meant to say . . . I remember. Many items now are better than before. Diseases eliminated, lifespans extended, great advances in, oh, agriculture, science . . . whatever. But are we any happier as a race? Assuming happy is a good thing. Are you any happier, love?"

"It's not a happy trade, a poet's . . . "

He sighed. "Our lives are immeasurably more comfortable than they once were. But—zero increase in happiness. We must pretend to be happy. But 'being modern' increases frustration, depression—it has brought on a satisfaction-shortfall. Look around you!"

"At least we now try to look after you elderly folk . . . "

He gestured. "Glance around you at this dump, Jean. Most of us are mad—including me . . . "

I kissed his hand. I hated Hull's honesty, I grieved for him.

Moderns on Ancient Ancestors

The main gallery of the Beijing Anthropological Research Institution was larger than Sir Gerald Fox and his entourage had expected. Having no external windows, it was lit only by bars of bright overhead lighting.

This lighting had been supplemented by a table on which a sculpted lamp burned. Below the lamp were bottles and glasses.

A company of five persons, one of them female, entered from the far reaches of the gallery. The senior man, dressed in a lounge suit, was introduced as Doctor Sen Hung Mai. He shook hands with Sir Gerald, welcoming him in faultless English.

"Will you take wine, sir?" Doctor Sen enquired.

A servant was summoned. Both men sat down and took a glass of wine. "This is a Kunming sauvignon blanc, from the south," Sir Gerald was told. He liked it moderately well.

"As you will know, Doctor Sen, I am in Beijing to sign our vitally important treaty of friendship between the peoples of your country and mine. From this day onwards we shall be linked, not only by politics and economics, but in other diverse and perhaps more congenial ways. Sport, entertainment, travel, science and indeed"—here he twinkled as he pronounced the word—"romance." The rest of the small company smiled.

"It indeed is a welcome and historic coming together of our peoples." Dr Sen was speaking formally but with warmth. "Such are the many favourable contacts we already enjoy. It is to our great profit—not merely financial profit—that we would wish to be so bound."

Sir Gerald was about to respond in turn, but Dr Sen suddenly launched into a new phase of discourse. He requested his distinguished English visitor to consider the length of time during which West and

East had been separate worlds, with no communication between them. His belief was that approximately thirty centuries ago the peoples in North Africa, those called Berbers, had begun to quit Africa for more productive lands to the north. He would like, if he might, said Dr Sen, to dwell upon the different fates those wandering tribes had met with. Some elected to head westwards, while others moved to the East.

The westerners in their wanderings eventually entered the lands that were to become known as Europe. All was densely afforested. By that time, the tribes had domesticated dogs and goats. They hunted deer and other animals until scarcity of food sources caused them to move on. As it happened, the goats ate the trees springing up as saplings, so that the land behind them remained more or less cleared as they per force moved on.

"And so finally," said Dr Sen, gesturing with a hand to reinforce that finality of which he spoke, "These groups were debarred by the ocean from further advance. They had to settle."

The climate, he said, was harsh, the soil had not long been broken. Some tribes turned back or forged south. Others, more sturdy, captured and tamed the wild horse. The horses could be broken to pull a plough, which a man could steer from behind with two wooden handles. So they learnt to grow crops which yielded a rough bread.

"Later, they invented a metal blade for their plough, which cut the soil better and deeper," said Dr Sen gazing down at the floor as if he imagined it to have been recently visited by one of his ploughs."

"It is a remarkable history as you tell it," said Sir Gerald, concealing a slight impatience. "Who can tell what they got up to during that period?"

"But you can see what follows," said Dr Sen gently. He went on to explain. He said that here was formed a remarkable linkage: man, animal, machine. Here lay the beginning of the remarkable cultures of the West.

The hospitable Chinese leader summoned a servant to refill their glasses, while remarking to his visitor, "But you will be eager to hear me discuss what happened to certain groups who quit Africa and travelled not Westward but Eastward."

"And what of those groups who fared Eastwards?" Sir Gerald asked obligingly.

Dr Sen, with a time-honoured gesture, gave a single clap of his hands.

At once, a side door opened. Three dancing girls emerged. The two flanking dancers were dressed in light frilly clothes; the dancer who danced between them wore next to nothing but a slender dark slip. This dancer was commandingly beautiful.

The trio came to a halt facing Dr Sen and Sir Gerald, whereupon this middle dancer began to recite in a musical voice.

"Here's something special we must face—
"The westward-farers found the perfect place.
"So here's our ancient oldest news:
"While you had your ploughs
"We had our bamboos.
"With bamboo you can train
"A clump to form you a thatched hut—
"Or cut one laterally . . . it makes a perfect drain . . . "

"So, if you please, our forebears took their ease.
"Of course in time we all have enemies—
"You beat your ploughshares into swords—
"How many wars West tribes fought
"Well, no one can recall . . .
"When we East folk faced enemies—barbarian, untaught—
"We simply built a wall!

The singer, smiling, ceased to sing. Her two companions backed away, still dancing, to disappear through the door through which they had come.

The lovely singer, however, stepped lightly forward and sat herself upon a startled Sir Gerald's lap. Smiling into his face, she ran her fingers through his thinning hair.

"Is this the welcome you show all visitors?" gasped the diplomat.

"This is a special occasion," said the Chinese. "Thank you, Mei Xiao," addressing the singer. "Good song, charmingly sung."

Silence prevailed for a while in the great chamber. Then Dr Sen spoke, to begin rather hesitantly.

"You see, there are those who claim that had this great separation continued for—well, for a few centuries more, then the division between

East and West would have been subject to evolutionary pressure. That would have resulted in there being two sub-species, unable to reproduce one with the other."

"You don't have to believe that," said Sir Gerald, in a scoffing tone.

"And what would have followed?" Dr San continued. "Well, coition between the two sub-races would still have been possible, but no fertility, no issue—really as if a lion lies with a tiger."

"Pffff," Sir Gerald said. "These old legends . . . "

He tightened his grip on Mei Xian's delectable waist . . .

The Hungers of an Old Language

"Was that a goat?" Ken asked. "A goat of a kind, with long shaggy coat and immense grooved horns . . . "

Ken Bekerwire's village was perched between mountain and sea. As the mountain was high, so the sea was deep, in a continuous narrative of geology. In this isolated place, Ken made a living from fishing, as his father had done before that and his grandfather before that.

His grandfather had been killed in a war fought for the country he hardly knew; Ken's father too died in a foreign place, fighting for the country he hardly knew. Ken had been spared war, but now fish were scarce and he felt old age drawing in upon him like a tide.

In the lusty days of his youth, Ken had once been prompted to climb the mountain behind the village. A boulder from the heights had trundled down to land in his vegetable patch, and he had taken it as a messenger. There were messages in all things.

At the top of Mount Greyharn he had found a thatched cottage. From this cottage had come a shy maiden, very slender, whose quiet beauty posted at once to Ken's inner feelings. This was Sheela Bawn Graay. The two of them had talked and talked until he kissed her lips and took her down with him into his village. When the sun cast the shadows of sunset on everything, she cried that she was so thin. She was starving, starving. What food was there on a mountain top this far north?

He took her to the little inn and piled her plate with potatoes and the meat of goats. "I am not greedy," she declared. She gave a brave smile. "There is so little to eat up on the mountain. Once I had two hens, but they died of winter cold. Some birds' eggs I can find in season. Otherwise, well, a bird perhaps. Even a snake . . . Or a fox if I am lucky . . . "

All people on earth—and it may well be the same elsewhere—have a secret history as well as an ordinary history, marked by passing years; some folk are barely aware of that inward history. But as he lay in bed with an arm about his slender new bride, Ken listened to what Sheela had to say of her inward story, of which he knew nothing.

And in her story of long ago, this mountain—her mountain—and all the land behind it had been elsewhere, and were joined to the great continent which now stood a long way distant, separated by the deep seas.

To break her fast in the morning, he cooked her the mackerel he had caught previously, and she ate with joy, laughing at her own greed, laughing and weeping because she had grown so thin.

Still her story went on, unwinding over the table.

According to Sheela's tale, great swords of ice had come, sawing up the land, and behind them rushed arms of the sea, and so the two lands had become and remained severed.

"But I, through my long parentage, retain knowledge of those distant times," she whispered to him, pressing her dainty breasts against his great chest. "And I retain knowledge of the Old Language." She gave a little whispered laugh. "It's said you cannot speak the Old Language unless you're starving."

"How's that?" he asked, perplexed.

"I was told the Old Language was never spoken when ruined by fat in the lungs or stomach. You cannot imagine how hard was life in the days when the Old Language was everywhere spoken."

"Speak it to me," Ken whispered. He felt that some vital unknown knowledge was to be passed to him—to him who knew so little beyond the times of tides.

So Sheela—or more properly, she said, Sheelagh—broke into a chant, where vowels were misty and consonants many, and filled with ancient music. The effect was more like a stifled cry than ordinary speech as spoken in the village. And so Ken fell under this lady's spell and feared her almost as much as he loved her. Because this song, this speech, came from a distant land and time immeasurable, to be caught in Sheelagh's delectable throat.

He asked her how old was this strange tongue she spoke.

"I only know it's older than is my mountain." she told him.

So they passed many months, body to body and mouth to ear.

As he lay beside his mysterious Sheelagh, Ken was the one who witnessed how her ribs showed under her pale flesh, and how thin were her arms, and how flat her stomach; truly, she was one woman able to speak the Old Language.

And he recalled during the pleasures of their love-making something his father had said—his father, gaunt and hairy, sitting in a creaking bamboo chair—"Poverty is the natural state for humanity. Wealth starts in the stomach and corrupts it . . . "

The natural state for humanity? Ken did not know. Indeed, he knew no one who was not poor—meaning, half-starved. It was a fairy tale to him that there were rich people . . .

At one time, he invited his neighbours to enter his room to listen to Sheelagh singing one of her ancient songs. And two old crones of the village, huddled in a corner of the room, nodded their grey heads and said, "Indeed, yes, it is no less than the tongue once spoken from a distant age, when plentiful fish gleamed like a spill of diamonds in a new sea . . . "

But the fish were no longer so plentiful. Generations of fishermen, including Ken's father and his grandfather, had diminished the stocks. Many people in the village now went hungry, near starvation, to eat but twice in the week, because of the shortage of fish.

No one could understand where the shoals of mackerel had gone. They could never believe that those same shoals had disappeared into village stomachs. It was that same appetite that had caused the Old Language to die away.

A day came when Sheelagh, obeying a mysterious summons, climbed back up the mountain to her deserted cottage, She went slowly, and when she arrived at that stark old homestead, she lay on the floor and with pain delivered a small baby daughter, showing a wisp of red hair, matching in tone Sheelagh's own ample curls.

And Sheelagh cried and nursed her baby, cried because she had fulfilled a vital part of a woman's destiny—and the baby did not then cry with her, but smiled its tiny unrehearsed smile.

When this dear new child cried, imagining the challenges of life ahead of her, then Sheelagh believed it was in the Old Language that she cried—as her mother had told her she had once done. As she had then needed milk, so did her infant now.

As for Ken, he seized on the opportunity of his beloved girl's absence to launch his boat and sail for deeper waters, where he hoped to find shoals of those elusive fish which were starving his village.

This was an uncertain day, misty, hovering between changing seasons. Ken scarcely knew where he was heading.

Rain set in, only to die away towards the horizon like an old blown shawl. But out of the murk ahead, Ken's keen eyes picked out land looming.

He knew there was no land anywhere near, not within half a thousand miles, as his father had said. This was just a small island, a wart upon the tousled sea. He made for its shelter with a feeling almost of terror, for here was strangeness indeed.

A gull came and cried its inscrutable regretful call before disappearing into a cloud sailing above the land.

Ken moored in what passed for a bay and lowered his nets—into which mackerel swarmed in joyful abandon. He hauled his catch on to deck and then (because he was not as young as he had been some years ago), went and lay down upon a patch of sandy beach to rest, and indeed to sleep.

In his slumbers he thought he heard some words of the Old Language his Sheelegh had taught him. He woke, sat up, and found to his terror a horned beast standing over him, horned and bearded and immense. It backed away, while regarding him with strange goat eyes. Its horns curling backwards to its shoulders.

"Fear not, Two-Legged one!" It spoke in a mere whisper, and the words too were of the Old Tongue, or very like.

So the pair of them were together, man and animal. Other goats came and gathered at a respectful distance. Both male and female came, and one female goat had with her a small offspring, as if to mirror the child to which Sheelagh had just given birth, many a league distant.

The goats spoke only in whispers and imperfectly, brokenly. But Ken's understanding was little better.

Nevertheless, as the great daylights of the noon wore away and the Earth turned its shoulder from the sun, he gained—or thought he gained—an understanding of an old history, as recounted by these animals gathered about him. Long long ago, immeasurable lifetimes past, so they told him in their bleating whispers, the hominids (meaning mankind) had domesticated an animal. That animal was the Ancestral Goat, which voluntarily went into partnership with the hominids. Those were long past golden years, when all the trees in the forests bore fruits—more than could be eaten—and the world was nothing but forests, green, dark green and untrodden.

Alas, in all stories, even those whispered by a herd of goats, what is halcyon must pass away as desolation dawns. So it was in those olden days. Matters could not be understood. Floods, rains, pestilence, starvation—the earth shaking, in order to remove the irritants of life upon its surface.

So survivors had fled, hominids and goats, all . . . Long whispered talk about this bad time, during which some of the goats present here on this drab spot wandered off to find and eat the seaweed to which their tastes had adapted.

It seemed that those survivors of their early fathers had come in their flight to the end of land. Seas and storms had rushed in. Darkness had prevailed. Those few who lived through this punishing time found themselves—what was that word?—Ken knew it not—'stranded' on this island. So they lived through the harsh centuries, talking the old talk, eating seaweed, or the odd fish trapped in pools. They awaited a hominid who would come and rescue them and restore them to wider pastures.

Much of this Ken understood, or thought he understood. But what was all goathood when set against his lovely Sheelagh? He fancied that if he did not soon get back to his home port, someone would raise the cry 'Lost at Sea', and his love would be anguished. So he laced up his boots and stood to bid the talkative goats farewell.

"Oh no," said they, with mighty tossings of horns. "You are the hominid that has come to save us. We will not let you go away. You must take us all to those broader pastures which we crave—which we have ever craved!—where there is no more seaweed, and trees yield the golden pear and little saplings wince to our very sharp teeth . . . "

And what was more, they showed Ken those very sharp teeth.

Sharp teeth, magnificent curved horns, devil's eyes . . . All set against him, with the horns rasping his thighs.

But Ken had his wits to rely on. He stood firm against his captors and spoke a few words in the Old Language.

"Indeed, I am come to rescue you. But you see that my boat is small. It would sink under your combined weights. I order that two of you are to accompany me now to my land. There we will assemble many boats to sail and rescue you all. You will be welcome in my land, with many green things to eat."

"What does the hominid say?" the horned animals asked each other, shuffling in their confusion.

One said, "Let us kill the hominid now and seize his boat."

Although the suggestion was popular, the wiser goats among the crowd had to confess that none of them knew how to sail a boat.

At last an understanding was reached. Ken was allowed back on to his ketch, with two animals preceding him there.

He stood stolidly in the stern, clutching an oar, staring at the small army of horned animals which now came from the beach to wade into the waters and watch him sail away.

"What if he fails to come back?" one old goat asked. But others immediately set upon him.

"You can always trust a hominid," they said.

The engine started up with a roar, frightening those animals who were up to their hocks in water; they stampeded to safety. Soon the island from which Ken had escaped was lost in a gathering mist. It might seem the little boat now floated alone in a world of water. The two goats folded their hooves under them and crouched flat on the deck, jaws against the planking, evidently affrighted by the immense unfolding of waves surrounding the vessel on all sides.

Evening was drawing in with a light scatter of raindrops when land came in sight, together with the village in which Ken and Sheelagh lived. Ken cut the engine and they drifted into port. Candle light showed in a window or two of nearby houses.

And who should be standing there, awaiting him as he docked? Why, his dear wife Sheelagh, holding in her arms her little newborn child.

Ken skipped ashore, tied up the boat and ran to embrace her, calling her his dearest darling, kissing her and the head of the baby with that ginger curl on top.

Sheelagh caught sight of two goat faces peering anxiously over the side of the recently moored boat. She was momentarily horrified.

She emitted a small shriek, clutching her husband more tightly, asking him with tremulous voice, "What have we there?"

To which, still clutching her, now laughing, he uttered the one word, "Food!"

How High is a Cathedral?

I was walking about my garden, thinking of my foolishness and of the past. My Rambling Rector had climbed and now covered the windows of my bedroom.

When I awoke of a morning, I could scarcely see out. Had that been the case: that I had never really seen out? Yet I had travelled widely.

I was thinking of an error made when in the Soviet Union, quite a while ago . . .

Part-funded by the Child Relief Company and part by elements of the Catholic Church, I was working in Malta to organise a Child Shelter unit. On several occasions, I took a ferry over to the small nearby island of Gozo.

Gozo, strange Gozo, had a little prehistoric park and an old church. The inhabitants wanted a cathedral.

Great ambition, small island! Yet somehow, over the years, money for building a cathedral filtered through. I was told that much of the cash was sent from abroad, from the pockets of workers labouring somewhere in Mediterranean lands.

This new cathedral was being built round the old church, where services were still being held. I attended several services there, a dark little holy place becoming surrounded by the clean stonework of this new manifestation of the worship of God.

This dedication was to be wondered at. Many Maltese builders worked on the new building without pay.

What was more, they determined to build the tallest cathedral in the world, taller even than St Paul's in England or St Peter's in Rome.

In the end, the marvel was accomplished. Then the small church encompassed within was demolished and carried away, stone by stone, plank by plank.

When my work in Malta was established, my superiors directed me to Russia, then the more sinister Soviet Union. Our hopes were limited. The authorities regarded any Child Shelter, even one run by Russian women, as somehow a British listening post.

At one point in our protracted negotiations, we were told that rooms might be available in Leningrad.

I developed a lustreless tolerance for Leningrad; the grand Winter Palace was stocked with splendid works of art. But the rooms we had been promised turned out to be just one room of a hall in some barracks. Negotiations were carried on sometimes at shouting level.

When I had a day off duty—this after two weeks in Leningrad—I decided to join a city tour. There were English people in our group; I found their talk soothing; they chuckled quite a lot. They even groaned quietly at some of the over-glorious claims made by our guide.

This guide was a rather attractive woman in her forties (as I supposed) who moved us on from talking point to talking point at a reasonable pace.

Near the metro station stood the Church of the Annunciation, ruinous, under repair.

"This cathedral has the third largest spire in the world," said our guide.

I raised a hand in protest, "Sorry, miss, but the cathedral on Gozo has the third largest spire in the world. This ruinous church here could therefore be at best the fourth largest . . . "

"Gozo? We not know of it. Nonsense!"

Of course I should never have spoken. And the Russians and their allies set up a howl against me.

Next morning as I was dressing, two men in uniform broke into my hotel room. I was accused of denigrating Russian architecture. Also of insulting the guide-woman.

I was marched off. Of course the trial came to nothing; our Embassy had a man to speak for me. But Child Shelter became a lost cause.

Such past things came to my mind as I walked in my garden.

A Middle Class Dinner

Oh, it was going to be such a lovely dinner. Digby Stackpole's cook had excelled herself. After an appetiser of whitebait, we were served with an inviting turkey, accompanied by bowls of various vegetables. Then followed a most brilliant pie, the pastry crust concealing blackberries, apricot and apple—all these dishes suitable for an autumn evening.

And all, of course, accompanied by a sauvignon blanc from New Zealand, or a good red from Boulogne, whichever one preferred.

Eight of us sat round the groaning board: our host, Digby Stackpole, at the head of the table, two neighbours, Larry Frobisher and his wife, the actress, Judy Raven, the solicitors, Terry and Jean Mullen with their grown-up son, Eric, and my wife, Laura Jane, and I.

Even before the whitebait had been consumed and the first sips of wine taken, Frobisher started talking about how his and Judy's two sons had become Soul Members of the Coptic Cross and had cycled to Berlin and back without once getting off their bicycles.

Terry Mullen burst into laughter. "Didn't they piss themselves?" he asked. Jean, his wife, exclaimed "Oh, Terry!" before laughing herself.

Laura Jane and I joined in the laughter.

Stackpole from the head of the table, said, "No need to be coarse, thank you, Terry. I doubt if any of us could cycle to Berlin and back. It needs stamina. The Frobisher twins were trying to raise money for the unfortunates of our society. Isn't that so, Larry?"

Frobisher, looking serious, addressed the table. "Poverty is a serious matter. As is discrimination. Sadly, we live in a corrupt society. Judy and I feel proud that our sons, inspired by the lessons of the Coptic Cross, raised almost two thousand pounds by their courageous ride. That money goes to those for whom we grieve, who suffer and are destitute . . . "

For some while he talked on in this vein, while those of us who felt we had been crass, if not actually amusing, looked serious and picked at our turkey.

It was Terry again who broke into laughter.

"Oh, come on, Larry, relax! The destitute and the skivers can look after themselves this evening . . . we don't need a lecture. Relax. Have a glass of the red."

"I am relaxed, thank you," said Frobisher, lapsing into a gloomy silence.

His wife spoke up, smiling at those around her. "This is such a nice evening, and such a lovely meal Digby has given us. Let's all be happy. I'm happy because I have just completed my run in that dreadful TV series, 'Crystal Balloon'. . . "

"Yes, well done, Judy," I said, though gossip was—I had had it from Facebook—that Judy Raven had been kicked off the show for lax interest and attendance.

Digby said, "I've never watched it." Then, perhaps thinking this might seem unkind to Judy, added, "Not my cup of tea, I fear . . . "

Judy made no response but, turning to Jean Mullen, sitting next to her, asked her how her garden was.

Jean looked flustered. "Oh, it's a bit weedy, I suppose . . . "

"As we all are, these days," said her husband, trying to be bright.

"Religion helps us keep a balance," said Frobisher. "But I suppose I'd better not go into that . . . "

Young Eric Mullen, who had hardly spoken now said, "Yes, indeed, better not! Some of us think all religions are foolish and cause trouble . . . "

"Not at all," began Frobisher, but his wife kicked him under the table and he fell silent. "Lovely meal," he muttered.

Laura Jane and I walked part of the way home with the Mullens. "A typical middle class occasion," said Terry.

"Enjoyable but bloody awful . . . "

Flying Singapore Airlines

Yes, Singapore Airlines delivered me to Cambodia, and a bus took me on to Angkor Wat.

Angkor Wat . . . that extraordinary orchestration of temples and other buildings . . . built in the early days of the Twelfth Century by edict of King Suryavarman. The great Khmer temple was at first Hindu, later becoming Buddhist. Mystery has always surrounded it.

My dreams washed against its venerable walls for many decades. Now here I stood, made penniless by those dreams, hardly daring to enter such an ancient, such a mysterious, creation.

In the heat, the great structure appeared to shimmer, as if some magic would cause it at any moment to disappear. I hastened my step, daring. I was alone. I entered in.

And immediately the sole of my left shoe came loose. Knowing I should have had it repaired, I knelt down, right knee on the worn stone, to see what I could manage. That posture as if in prayer.

A woman's voice came to me, a tremor, a whisper.

"I see you are at prayer, as many many have been before you, in thirst for it. Come, I will take you up . . . "

I stood. She stood before me, dark eyes fixing mine. She was dressed in a pale heavy gown. One naked arm was raised to carry a small flickering lamp.

It seemed to me she said that she would take me before the 'Psalm King'. She turned and moved forward, through a narrow entry I had not previously noted. All helpless now, I followed. Mouth open. Hypnotised.

We walked in a mysterious darkness, lit only by this fair creature's light. Suddenly we were among many—oh, countless!—people, and I was moving, dancing with them. Oh, how light I was!—and shoeless! Renewed!

See how the temple's lighted.
No more are we affrighted . . .

Music—I could not be sure if it was Song—seemed to percolate about a tenuous figure ahead. When I asked if this was the Psalm King, as mentioned in the lost realms, she, and not she alone, said they had no kings here: psalm king was what they were doing—being like notes to Vishnu's music.

No kings, no broken shoes—

Suddenly, immensely, I moved with a consort of others into a side chamber where all was still. Those with me seemed insubstantial, and more vivid, more 'real' for all that.

Oh, I—what was I now? I had become free of my old concerns, of my petty ills and vices, my loss, my struggles about money, the vexations of tyrannical political systems . . . of many such things I could now—whatever 'now' meant—no longer remember.

"You have closed the door on them. Here, here in this olden golden place you have only your Self . . . "

"For such is the true realisation of—" Did they say Buddhism, or did they mean Buddhism?

I was Psalm King with this select multitude, and the fine grave woman was speaking—or was it a chant?—of how the centuries with their burdens of war, revolution, poverty and injustice had worn down humanity until humanity was unable to recognise its own burdens, but must walk for ever down its worn streets.

Here in an older freer dimension, there was as they said, only the Self, a softened one item in a sea of truly human humanity.

And where had I come from on that expensive elegant plane? Had there once been a city called Liverpool? A city . . . A city . . . I saw the absurdity, the cruelty, of it and a million places like it.

"Did I want to go back?" she asked, laughing.

"Back?" I said. "I don't know what it means." Laughing.

The Apology

Harry Cardman was gardener to the Mainbergs of Helizburg House, a grand mansion in the midlands of England.

Luck came Cardman's way when he featured in a BBC TV programme on gardening. He appeared only for four or five minutes by his brother's count (his brother Ken was an accountant), but in that time said something intelligent about clematis plants.

The Mainbergs happened to be watching the programme. Realising that his gardener had some intelligence, a quality he deemed not particularly necessary in gardeners, Sir Thomas Mallory Mainberg began to walk in his gardens and so chance to talk with Harry.

Harry was circumspect. He had no wish to lose his job; suspicious by nature, he reckoned that if he appeared to be becoming too friendly with the governor, the governor might come to resent it—and to sack him.

However, things changed when Mainberg enquired what exactly Cardman was growing in the small Daphne Greenhouse. The Daphne was named after an aunt-by-marriage, now dead, who in later life had become eccentric. The greenhouse named after her had remained derelict for some years, standing behind a giant clump of pampas.

Showing the governor into the greenhouse, Cardman explained that he had taken to growing daphnes in the greenhouse. It seemed appropriate.

"Ah, yes, daphnes, Cardman. Originally a Chinese plant."

"Yes, sir, Chinese. I have branched out, as you can see. I trust you'll not mind when I admit to growing other plants of Chinese origin in here—Jasmines, Corydalis, Lillies, Primulas . . . "

Mainberg leaned on his stick to look frowningly at his gardener. "You amaze me, Cardman. Why exactly this interest in China? Have you ever been to that extraordinary country?"

"No, sir, I have not had that good fortune. But I did spend some months working in Thailand—in the British Embassy grounds—and there I became friendly with Chinese people. I liked them greatly."

"I know the embassy in Bangkok. Extensive grounds . . . "

"Indeed, sir, but unfortunately over-run by hares. The local hare. At least when I was working there."

"Hares? Good heavens! Never knew that. Our ambassador never mentioned hares in my presence."

"No doubt he considered hares beneath his dignity, sir."

Mainberg gave what he considered was a curt nod and stomped out of the greenhouse. It never did to be too affable with the riff-raff he employed.

Thinning of hair, reddening of nose, and a recently worn addition of silver-frame spectacles, had given Mainberg a seedy look of late. Age having also bowed his shoulders, an unfriendly joker of a cousin had described Mainberg's appearance as that of a 'rain-soaked haystack'.

Moreover, age had been at another of its usual works, in failing to improve his lordship's temper. Now, sitting with his wife, Lady Caroline, over dinner at 8 p.m., he became grumpy at the approach of the sweet, a multi-coloured blancmange.

"Blancmange!" he exclaimed in disgust. "French word—send the bloody thing back to France. You know I loathe the stuff."

"It is one of cook's masterpieces," said Lady Caroline, in tones suggesting she liked the cook less than her husband liked blancmange, "Will you have some mince pie instead?"

When he consented to that proposal, she was moved to say that he seemed rather rarified this evening."

"Rarified? Rarified?" He admitted that he was rather out of touch, something on his mind he was unable to recall. That troubled him. Mind failing, mind going . . .

"I observe that you failed to brush your hair," said Lady Caroline, haughtily.

Mainberg smote the table top. "Yes, that's it, of course! Hare! Hare . . . the gardener chap, Cardigan, was waffling on about hares . . . "

Smiling in an awful way, he began to tell his wife a story, ignoring the mince pie, accompanied by a bowl of brandy butter which the butler had brought in.

"It was my second tour of duty in China. You weren't accompanying me. No doubt you were back here in Tessingford, taking it easy and bearing another child . . .

"Anyway, I was doing my stuff in the province of Szechuan. This was the year after Chairman Mao had died—whatever year that was. I was talking in a small town when a woman came up to speak to me. She had just begun to operate a small new radio-broadcasting station and was having trouble with local authorities. Oh yes, her name was Shu Chei. I remember it now. A good-looking young woman. Hmm.

"One of Mao's edicts had been that children of richer classes should go to live with the peasants for a while and so learn country skills and manners.

"Shu Chei and three of her friends—all of good families—were then in their last year at finishing school when they were ordered to go and muck in and learn among the peasants.

"There had been a culture in Szechuan fifteen centuries before Jesus Christ. The four young ladies found that the peasants had scarcely advanced since then. In fact, the confounded peasants were cruel and filthy. Filthy and cruel . . .

"These ruffians hated to be stuck with four educated young women who had superior manners and knew nothing of country matters—such as, for instance, how to castrate a goat. Essential for all right-thinking persons.

"To punish the unfortunate newcomers, they were given damn all to eat. They had to live off the gross remains of a peasant meal, or to eat grass, or the blooms or fruits of certain shrubs. They were reduced to starvation level and could hardly drag themselves about. And that formed a motivation for more persecution.

"A lesson there for all of us, Christine, old girl. Being poor is a loathsome state to be in, not at all the halcyon state the Romantics portray it as. *Never vote Labour* . . .

"Shu Chei was eventually driven to construct a little trap, fashioned with the flexible outer branches of a willow tree. They wove a cage of sticks. The girls set this contraption on a bank near where they slept. By this time the peasants had rejected them and left them alone.

"They awoke next morning at dawn. Lo and behold, what had they caught in their trap!? Why, a well-fed young hare, struggling to get free. Two of the girls hurriedly gathered up litter and started a fire on which they could cook the creature. Shu and the other girl dragged the hare from the cage, keeping a firm grasp of it, no matter how hard it struggled.

"They looked at the hare and saw how beautiful it was, how frightened its eyes were.

"They kissed it and petted it. And—mark this!—they apologised that they had to kill it so that they might live..

"All four of those girls wept as they strangled that hare . . . "

Mainberg fell silent. A tear stood in his eye.

"I've never forgotten all that," he said. "Do we ever offer up an apology for all the animals and fish we kill and eat?

"Doesn't that tell you something about Chinese culture? Isn't it superior to ours? . . . Those poor starving girls . . . "

"Yes," said Lady Christine. "And of course you have told me that dreary tale many times before . . . Get on with your pudding, dear."

Camões

Oh well, here goes. May as well tell all. . . .

I call myself Corler. I'm a traveller. Better still a scraveller. Always on the move. This drops in your Facebook from a place in Malaysia called Putrajaya. An okay place. Bear in mind I'm now pretty ancient. Not quite up to a lot of things I used to be up to (he sniggered.)

Once I wrote a book. A pamphlet let's say. Entitled it 'The Quest for Choot' I had read a book called 'The Quest for Corvo' and I was hanging out on the coast of Southern India. I had had a woman a night for how long? Then this one.

She liked to lift up her skirts and flaunt what she called her Choot. Don't know how you spell it. Never found it in any dictionary I looked into. But I did recognise this admirable object when I looked into *it*.

By and large, women all round the world are shy—or let's say cagey—about letting a guy see their cosy little choots. Yet isn't it what every man dreams of at least every day—maybe every hour?

So my little pamphlet came out and received only one review . . . That's how a scraveller lives. Disappointment, hand to mouth, if the hand's not on that particular little item. Or the mouth, come to that. Some taste much better than others,

There I was, lolling about on the Malay beach. I'd been in the bazaar for something to eat—a crab, in this case. Then I had happened on a guy selling carpets and such gear and he had a line-up of used books for sale. Among the clutter there was just one book printed in English, a book torn and tattered and called 'Epic and Poems of Camões'. I bought it. It cost nothing.

I have to tell you this guy was or had been a celebrated poet in his day.

He was called Luís de Camões, and he was Portuguese. Read on . . .

The guy who wrote a preface to the book said that Camões had been compared to some of the Greats, Shakespeare, Dante, Homer. Lucky those three greats didn't write in Portuguese, otherwise you wouldn't have recognised their names. Christ, maybe you didn't recognise their names as it is—the damned world has become so illiterate. Have *you* ever watched a Shakespeare play performed on stage?

'Hamlet', let's say. Come on, be honest.

Well, to get on with it, this Camões chap wrote an epic entitled 'The Lusiads'. Seems it was a tale of adventure and wanderings on a grand scale. Instant appeal where I was concerned. And I read that he had died way back in 1580. On June 10th. Happened I was reading this on the last day of May. So, ten days to go.

I went to the university in KL, to ask about Portugal. I did not fancy going to Europe. World War 2 was barely over and I believed the whole place was still strewn with dead bodies.

This academic was helpful. He could look things up, and he phoned through—and found there was a steamer leaving Singapore on the morrow which would actually call in at Macau (a trading port, he said) on the 8th next.

I got myself down to Singapore pronto and—good luck that—managed to hire myself out as a deck hand for the trip.

You know how it is. I don't have to tell you. The lousy old steamer got engine trouble and put into a Chinese port for a quick repair job. We arrived in Macau on the 11th . . .

My plan was I thought Camões sounded like someone I could write a short thing or two, or possibly even a book about. Someone might be interested.

Chinese types were sweeping glittering stuff from streets. Something in the way of celebration had been going on.

In a handy bar, two Brit squaddies were drinking. I joined them and asked if there had been celebrations for Camões' death. "We was on duty in barracks yesterday," one of them said. "Missed all the fun. Some Portuguese bloke, wasn't it?"

"Wanna drink?" the other asked. So we got into the serious stuff. They were cheerful company, and they knew what Choot meant, amid laughter. Then they had to report in, back to barracks.

Directly I was outside in the hot air, I felt badly squiffed.

Tottering, I grabbed a post. A great vacant space loomed indistinctly before my eyes.

Lots of space . . . Ahead a line of trees along a waterfront. Houses behind me. I staggered over to the trees, settling against one of them. I could sleep here—nowhere else to go.

Farther along, helped by the night, three guys coming single file my way, knives gleaming. Trees to cover their advance. I saw danger. But, so lethargic was I, I reckoned I could jump up at the last moment and scare them off.

Then, if you can believe it. . . .

A woman came running up from a corner house in the row behind, and grabbed me by the shoulders.

"You're in danger, love!," she told me. Really, I had been too smashed to cope.

This angel of avoirdupois got me to my feet and across the road, into the house where she lived. Slammed the door, swearing in her own tongue.

She lifted me into a sort of big cot, saying she'd get me a mug of tea. "You've had too much to drink," she told me. I'd never have guessed.

"They'd have robbed you and killed you, those bastards."

She pulled my clothes off without ceremony, saying "Lie down, man!" Some young girls in slips drifted along and had a look and a giggle.

Tea came. She held my head up as I drank. Then I faded out.

I woke at dawn with my saviour lady, stark naked, climbing into the cot on top of me. Seeing her big jovial choot looming, I got a good hard on. So we celebrated my survival.

This wonderful person accompanied me under the shower and then dried me vigorously. This brought about another turn of what she called jig-jig. Standing jig-jig this time.

After which, she kissed my cheek and showed me the door. They were opening for business.

It may have been about two years later I found myself back in Europe. I landed in Spain and hung about with an old aunt. Then something brought Camões back to mind. I managed to cadge some lifts and so at last found myself in Portugal. There stands a statue to Luis de Camões in Lisbon, and then later I found myself in a small town, having a drink in a certain Camões Square. And the drink came from the Café de Camões. So—not forgotten!

He sounds like a real winner. And—this has its appeal for me—some guy here tells me that Camões died in a ditch—poverty-stricken . . . the Great Portuguese Poet!

The Question of Atmosphere

The house and its setting were really not ideal places for a suicide.

Dr Geoge Handison, my celebrated uncle, owned three houses in England and one in Florida in the U.S.A. He had been a bacteriologist for the government, often working secretly, and had retired because of his illness.

One particular house stood almost on the cliffs, overlooking the beaches of a small town on the south coast of England. There my sister and I, and her two children, were staying for a month's holiday.

My Uncle George had no direct descendants. My sister Laura and I were the offsprings of Blanche, George's sister. Our mother at this time, though aged, was undergoing entangled divorce proceedings from father, her husband. That was why we were taking refuge with my uncle in that pleasant and calm situation on the cliffs.

My good uncle had begun to suffer from a number of medical problems, mental and physical; mother claimed that George had even begun to smell differently.

On this particular fateful morning, Uncle George stood on the porch and waved us goodbye. We drove off into town in my mother's Bentley. We were planning to do a little shopping, with the promise of the beach in the afternoon, when the tide would be out.

I should say something about Uncle George's illnesses. He had been experimenting with para-physicological factors, designed, so it was said in some quarters, to develop into secret neurological weapons, possibly for future government use.

When he found himself beginning to fall ill, uncle had gone secretly to the U.S.A. where he had a friend at Harvard Medical School. This friend was Harvey Blande. Blande believed he had a cure for George, and applied a number of drugs in fairly large doses to his patient. These included a period of sustained narcosis—which probably did Uncle George more harm than good. He was prone, *gone*, for ten or more days under this drug.

He described himself jokingly as 'walking wounded' but at one time, when he was in conversation with a local doctor, I heard him suggest that perhaps he was a victim of his own government, trying to brainwash him.

The predicament in which my Uncle found himself had many implied ramifications. Little I cared, I have to admit, since I was then just becoming very interested in a young woman who was so far eluding me.

So Laura and I were cheerful, popping in and out of shops with the children, who were on their best behaviour, particularly since Laura had dashed into a shop specialising in seaside gear, and had bought little Tim a large new inflatable boat, which we all planned to launch that very afternoon.

We enjoyed a light lunch served on a hotel patio, and then headed back to Lotus House, as was the name of my Uncle's home, with the new inflatable boat in the back of the Bentley.

Laura and I went to open the front door. Was there even then some kind of shadowy premonition? I mean, even before the brass doorknob was turned?

We entered the house.

The house was choked by something nameless, something still and horrible.

It is difficult to find words in the English language which can describe the impact of this sinister and unheralded atmosphere into which we entered, only to find ourselves submerged. The immediate consequence was to choke our throats and silence us. The boy, sensing nothing, ran about squawking.

We had fallen under the power of something spiritually poisonous. Although our sight was totally clear, we were stricken by this spiritual nastiness. The quality was experienced almost as a solid, intimating that something was extremely wrong here, in the house.

Laura's face had become ice-yellow. Without a word, she began to make her way slowly upstairs, moving like a machine. I made my way through the house, down the passage, into the kitchen—all the electric lights were burning through the daylight—where that deadly atmosphere was at its thickest, and proceeded as if drugged through a side door into the garage.

The garage was full of blood. That is, blood and brains. Scarlet brains hanging dripping from walls and ceiling.

Uncle George, in his final hour, had dragged a stool to the side of his car, wedging it between car and wall. He had taken two guns with him. Both guns had been loaded. He had used only one. Seated, placing the muzzle of the gun under his jaw, he had blown his brains out. His body now lay wedged between car and wall. I stood in paralysis.

A sound of a footstep. Laura was about to enter the garage.

"Laura," I said, with complete control of voice. "Please do not come in! Keep the children away. Uncle George has shot himself. There's a bit of a mess everywhere."

I was perfectly calm. I went back into the house to phone the hospital. I sat Laura down and poured her a drink. I sent the children, protesting, into the garden to play.

In due course of time, an ambulance with two paramedics arrived outside. I opened up the roll-top door of the garage and the medics managed between them to lift George's body out and stow it into their vehicle.

And then all the necessary rigmarole attending such a suicide of such a noted man rolled into place. Radio women and various reporters arrived to besiege Lotus House. How did we feel? they asked. There was the funeral, of course, attended by many people, including a group of men in black overcoats who spoke to no one. Solemn music was played. George's sister Blanche, my mater, wept discretely on my shoulder.

It is now a dozen years since George's suicide took place. Those two dear children of Laura's are now adults and going their own ways.

What haunts me is that terrible atmosphere engulfing us as we walked all unsuspecting into the house where my uncle had—within the hour—blown his brains out.

What could have projected that communication? What did it announce about something of which we have no knowledge?

Could it have been a kind of toxoplasma, activated by the report of the revolver?

Why—how—did it release a blanketing toxin of terror? Could it have been a primitive inheritance?

How did it spread throughout the house?

Where did it come from, if not from us. And where has it gone?

What exactly does it imply about submerged human mentalities of which so far we understand little and know nothing?

Illusions of Reality

Metal touched metal, gentle as a mother's kiss. Ron Don Cordwangler crossed from the ferry through the opening door into the zeepee. A welcome party stood awaiting him. Foremost or fivemost among that party stood CE Lulu Amiss. Lulu came forward and touched Cordwangler with a traditional gesture. It was warm but fleeting. She knew what he had come for... Although he had had his sel treatment, still he was unwelcome.

"We know what you wish to see" said Lulu. "You are Director of A-Z Zeepees Inc., isn't that so? The ferry-ride up here can disurb, so let's have a starberger first and then we'll leave you to sneak about in pieces.'

"I take it you mean 'peace'?" First sentence to Ron Don.

Pleased and displeased, he went with Lulu. She exuded a light stream of crimson BR—body radience. Otherwise, she was conventionally beautiful—zeemakapt, it was called. Long word for short story.

Together with their coffee they were brought platters of fresh-water jays. Enjoying the dish and Lulu's flow of data, Ron Don was aware of a living difference from Earth; he was unable to think what caused it.

Later, he roamed alone, throating various items back to A-Z in Colorado on Earth. He came to a well-tended garden space, with squares of vegetables and small pools. Ron Don was already aware of blue-winged birds overhead; they were more frequent here. He spoke to a gardener about them. The gardener was a spruce youth, tightly green coated.

"We are orderly here. Cannot afford not to be. All is miniature or minimalised," he said, smiling at Ron Don. "They breed in the microwood over there," He pointed with a hunched shoulder. "We have room on a zeepee for only one type of bird. The blue jay is pretty and is well-behaved, since it has no competition."

"And tastes good," said Ron Don.

"That'll be the variety that has become aquatic." He looked meditatively down at the ground. "Of course they are not real . . . None of us are. . . . You realise this Zeepee is an Illusion of the Reality Zone . . . We have whole-heartedly received the message of the master."

Not liking this turn in the conversation, Ron Don remarked that he felt himself to be real enough, at least for these few paragraphs.

"Of course," said the young gardener, to whom I as the writer of this fiction have not yet given a name. "It's such an immense relief to realise that we are not real, but mere figments of a Story. Or perhaps I should say 'The Story'. Our suffering is unreal—and our girl friends."

He gave a chuckle, scratching his crotch. "Life would not be possible here without sel or the teachings of the Great Neffin."

"Yes, admittedly Neffin was a great man, greater even than Leonardo da Vinci or Darwin." He disliked mentioning Neffin to a mere gardener, however talkative.

The gardener, still nameless, looked penetratingly at him.

"You may think I am young and only a nameless gardener—with a girl friend due any minute—but the interesting fact is that there were those who suspected the truth ages before Neffin came along."

Ron Don laughed and turned away. He caught sight through the window of the frigid continent of Antarctica they were orbitting. Was there in Neffin's great Story room for the huge barrens of Antarctica and Arctic, rendering at least a quarter of the planet uninhabitable under their dull ice? Or was the Story not yet complete? After all, people never spoke or thought of Neffin on the other zeepees. No more than Neffin had spoken of this uninhabitable realm of the world or page . . .

The gardener, caught Ron Don's arm and wrenched at it.

"Listen to me, Don Ron! I'm no fool. I've studied. Have you ever heard of Thomas Hobbes? He lived and philosophised in the seventeenth century. He got close to the Truth of Unreality even then."

Whereupon he began to recite from one of Hobbes' essays, while fixing Ron Don with a hazel-eyed glare. "'Whatsoever we imagine is Finite. Therefore there is no idea or conception of anything we call Infinite. No man can have in his mind an Image of infinite magnitude . . . '"

"Well . . . " said Ron Don, but the gardener would not be stopped, at least for the continuance of another paragraph.

"So then Hobbes goes on to claim in that same essay 'On Man', that

'When we say any thing is Infinite—like the South Pole you keep staring at—we signify only, that we are not able to conceive the bounds of the thing named, having no conception of the Thing, but of our own inability.'"

(I copied this from an old volume; therefore it must be true.)

By coincidence, as the gardener uttered the word 'conceive', the most beautiful girl one might conceive, never mind describe, came in view. Writers arrange such matters. She walked towards them along a path between pools where goldfish were busily evolving. More poetry than prose . . .

"Darling!" the gardener exclaimed, turning aside momentarily to say to Ron Don, sotto voce, "Actually, she's a bit of a bore . . . "

"Sweetheart!" the girl responded. She was closer now and more beautiful, eluding description. She kissed the gardener on his mouth.

"I had such a funny dream in the night," she lisped.

Ron Don said, "I'd better be getting on. More zeepees to come . . . "

He would have been surprised to learn that here his Story ends, Neffin or no Neffin. He was, let's put it this way, 'taken short'. . .

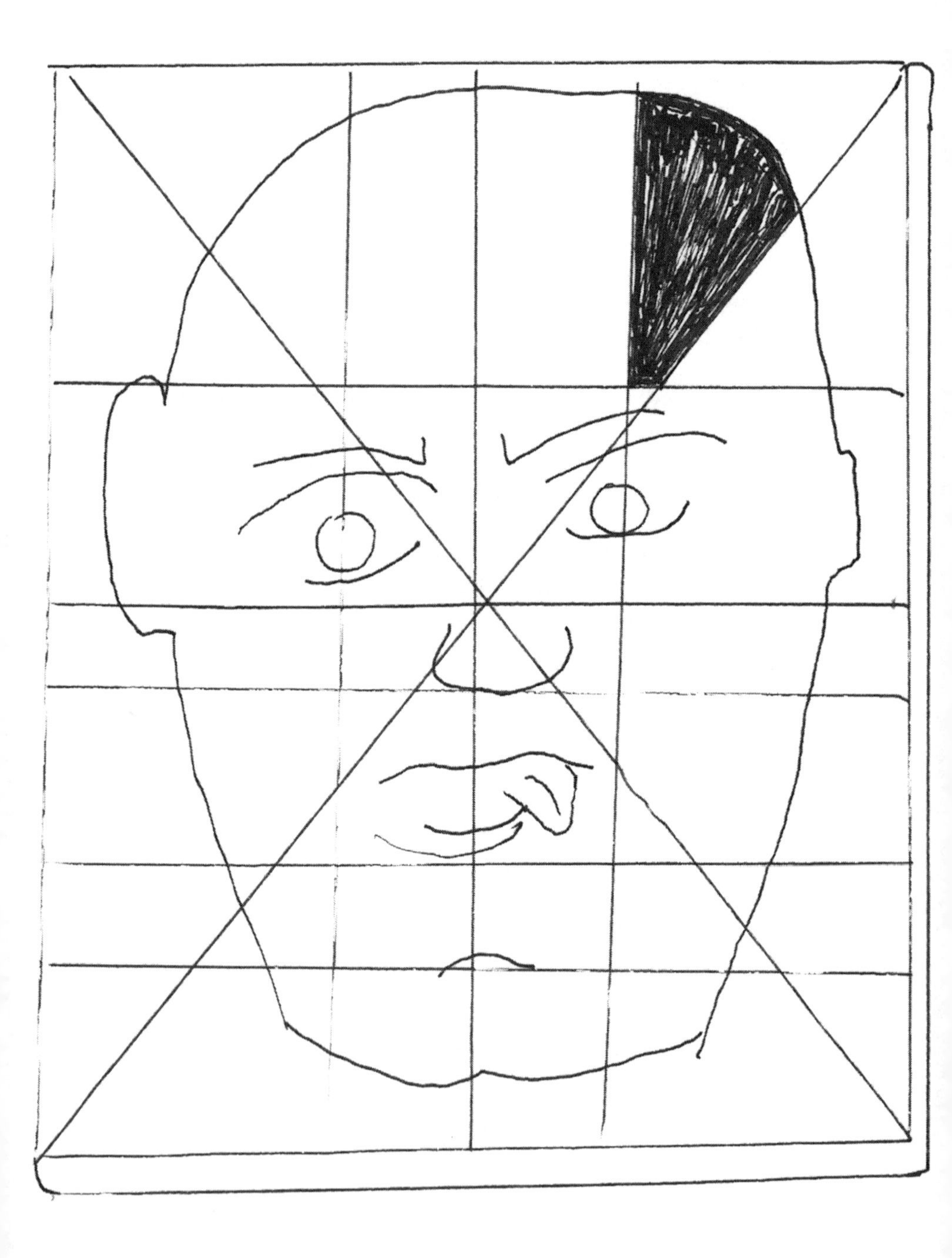

Lady With Apple Trees

While I'm eating this delicious apple, I want to talk of a woman I hardly knew. I admired her and her attitude to life. Forgive me, but I longed for her.

Firstly, a short prologue. My family, the Robertsons, were numerous and quarelsome. It was stocked with assertive cousins, aunts and uncles, together with old men of earlier quarrelsome generations. Many of them were prolific breeders.

Working as I did on railway systems, I cut myself off from these people. Indeed, the only one I knew well (and she I was deeply fond of) was Dorothea.

My grandfather, when late in his life—for in those bygone days before medicine had become a science, when to reach the age of seventy was to be old—had courted and married Dorothea della Cremone. She was a young Italian woman of distinguished family, as her name implies. She too had fallen out with her parents.

Grandfather and Dorothea were married in Gibraltar, to evade the physical disapprovals of both families.

So grandfather took his new bride back to his modest estate in Hampshire, where we suppose they were happy. Happy until the grand old boy took ill and died. They had enjoyed only two years together.

Dorothea did not return to Italy, as might have been expected. I sought her company frequently; we developed a close friendship. While I often took her bottles of champagne, she gave me something far more precious, the sense of a decent cultivated world where actions and behaviour could be assessed for their merits. The sense of a civilization to which we could all freely contribute.

Dorothea died unexpectedly in her sleep one night, to my sorrow. In her will, she left her house and grounds to me.

I moved there with wife and children. By this stage, Pam, my poor wife, was entirely given to snatches of conversation on Twitter and Facebook, punctuated only by bursts of television and Love Film.

Nothing more need be said of Pam. A flame had somehow gone out. Perhaps my severely mechanistic life was partly to blame. I had been working on a full-size replica of the LNER Class A3 locomotive, No. 4472 Flying Scotsman; the original had been built for the LNER in 1923 . . . But that of course is by-the-by.

FLYING AND BOMBING

Pete and Pauline Gibbs sat together by their fireside to watch the evening's television. It was Sunday. The main evening's programme was to be devoted to a famous writer. Neither Pauline nor Pete were interested in writers. They did not read books. But as it happened Pete had once met Anthony Hoskice, the subject of the forthcoming programme. Pete had fallen over in a London bar; Hoskice, leaving with a jolly party of people, laughing, had helped Pete to his feet, and they had joked briefly about the incident. It was the one time in his life that Pete Gibbs had encountered a famous person. He had always treasured the incident.

Hoskice came on screen smiling, wearing a velvet jacket over an open-neck shirt, the collar wings of which protruded.

"I've been walking with my producer along Madison Avenue, here in New York. Trying to decide what I should say and not say in my allotted hour. I love New York, it looks quite old nowadays.

"We all have ancestors, like it or not. What my ancestors did before my father was born I have no idea. I revered my pa, so capable and brave. The first I remember of him, my parents and I were out East and Mike, my pa, was flying for Chiang Kai Chek. Chiang Kai Chek was fighting Communists. While I don't actually remember Chiang in person, I do remember his wife. Madam Chiang was clever and beautiful. Her image appeared on Western postage stamps. My mother knew Madame Chiang slightly, and so I was introduced to her as a small boy.

"My father flew Chiang's planes, and bombed the rebels . . .

"So that's as it were 'my context'. Then everything fell apart. Second World War and all that. I was sent to boarding school in England. It was the last I saw of my beloved parents. Both of them were killed when Adolf Hitler's bastards bombed London.

"I started writing intensively while still at school and so I have continued ever since. I'm a steppenwolf.

"I guess you're familiar with the term steppenwolf? One who lives peaceably enough in society, yet knows he is alienated. He has come in from the steppes and is forever lonely. Isolated. I am fortunate in living with a dear companion—a lady also from outside our limited communities.

"You realise I am talking about my work, my novels, my stories. It's how I make contact. Some contact. An approach.

"Yes, I'd say that, and also a defence. My subject's disorder. Love and disorder. The secret chaos of even civilised societies. Not wickedness, not exactly weakness. There may be other planets of other suns a few light years from Earth, where it is possible for the beings there to live sensible and philosophical lives. Here—here—does that opportunity exist?

"Think back—if you are old enough—think back to last century, that famous Twentieth Century. Two world wars, utter fear and squalor, millions of corpses, two opposing armed forces run by the insane, Adolf Hitler and Joseph Stalin. Plus Chairman Mao later—

"Sorry! I'm getting a signal to stop this rant and talk about my books. To be nice . . .

"Well. My books are full of strangers. You the reader are introduced to them. Things happen to them; the end and we can find out no more about them. That's novels. Bones to pick . . .

"I enjoy writing short stories. Very few short stories are published, but that's beside the point. It's not the payment, it's the pleasure of crisp concision.

"An editor, sensible man, once told me that if I could not readily think of a title—or begin with a title—then that was proof the story was no good. How nice to have a simple sensible rule . . . There are no such rules for novels. The most stimulating novels—those by Franz Kafka, let's say—tend towards unresolved mystery. Fragments of a life like, we assume, Kafka's own life. Kafka, I'd imagine, was a steppenwolf, but don't take my word for it.

"Oh dear! In the wings they're holding up a placard which says, 'NEVER MIND KAFKA, TALK ABOUT CHARLES DICKENS.

"Well, thanks chaps, I see what you mean. Having published sixty books, I'm supposed to be a popular author. Not as popular as Dickens, of course. Yes, I used to read and love Dickens's writings, particularly 'Great Expectations'.

"Dickens has the Marshalsea. That great prison! Many of us live in great prisons without knowing it.

"Thank goodness, it seems my time is up. I hope you enjoy my various writings. Thanks for listening, if you have been."

Pauline Gibbs, switching off, said, "Well, that was a lot of waffle. I'll get us some supper."

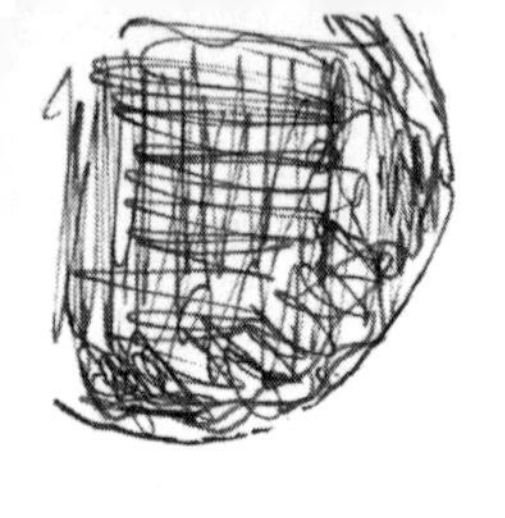

The Solar Disc floods through the minds of living kind and is gone

Molly Smiles Forever

I had been praying alone at the top of the cathedral's high tower. From that position, one can see on a clear day the towers of another distant cathedral. To my belief, our two cathedrals are the only ones in the world where one can see from one cathedral to another.

My thanksgivings shrank in my throat. A small cloud, at no great distance from where I knelt, had ceased to move across the sky. Two birds, probably blackbirds, hung suspended in the morning air, their wings spread. And the very air itself felt petrified. These impossibilities dried the words on my tongue.

I descended the creaking stair down to the nave, and through the southern transept. Not the slightest sound came up to me. In that total silence, I moved towards the southern gate. This entailed passing a little side-chapel wherein lay the tomb of a royal Angevin queen. The tomb had lain there since A.D. 1401.

As I made to pass, I discovered that the ghost of the queen had risen from her resting place. I halted, much taken aback. The royal spectre stood in my path, grey, grisly, transparent. It held aloft a lamp which glowed with a dull gleam, casting shadows over her countenance. I could see masonry through her flowing gowns.

Confessedly, I was alarmed. My voice sounded hollow to me when I spoke.

"I am your Archbishop." I said. "Return to wherever you came from!"

And behold, she was gone . . .

I walked on. The great pillars stood to either side, soundless. I chided myself for feeling some relief when I gained the street. But everything here too was soundless, motionless. A dog stood rigid on the pavement, jaws open, preparing to bark a bark that now would never sound.

It was but a short walk to my modest dwelling-place. I passed people caught in mid-tread—now eternally static, whatever their means or intentions had been.

My side-door opened for me. I went into the kitchen, where my wife sat at the kitchen table, little Mickey on her knee. Molly seemed to be reaching out for me, a smile of welcome on her face. I felt tremors of love inside me. I adored this dear woman so greatly, I sometimes feared I was on the verge of blasphemy.

What a sorrow to find my adored Molly as rigid as the rest of the world. Well, I tried to console myself, her dear smile would ever remain, unchanging.

I took a seat opposite her, wondering what I should do next. Should I venture to Westminster? But there too everything, everyone, would be inanimate.

And the flow of the Thames would be stilled. No boat would move on its surface.

Of a sudden, I was filled with an immense weight of love for England, precious England, that great store of experience, for all its masses and memories, now no more . . . Now, as it were, frozen, refrigerated.

Of course, I could kneel and pray. I got down on the matting by the oven. But what could I say to God—to our God who had allowed some cosmological accident whereby Time and its metronomic passage had failed?

Completely failed.

I remained on my knees, quite close to Molly, beloved Molly, with her fixed smile.

Days Gone By

A mist hung over the swamp where Dino lay tethered. Darkness had fallen.

At the doorway of a strongly-built straw hut, Kish-desh sat, nursing a newly born baby. Kish-desh's sexual quarters were still sore from the delivery. She fancied that Forg's driving into her, to leave his mess behind, had something to do with her pregnancy and the birth, but could not be sure.

Forg now sat by the eastern post of the camp. He was guard for this night, snoozing lightly on the raised platform under the trees. All the rest of the large family unit, including distant grandads and semi-aunties, were piled up, sleeping or twitching, in or near the hut.

It was warmer this night; the sheets of ice were retreating, withdrawing to the unknown north. Only the Moon, a sliced quarter, looked chill. Kish-desh feared it.

Forg let out a yell. Almost at once, men started to run from the hut, some with spears, some with cudgels, and after them women, Boice-lat with a drum which she swore would terrify and drive off any animal or monster.

This time, it was a monster Forg heard—one that made the saplings shake. He jumped about, shouting, waving his arms. He had caught a glimpse in the thickets of the tawny curse-beast, Tirro. Tirro smashed everything as he advanced. The males of the family knew—or believed they knew—that it was Tirro's destiny to break into the encampment and kill—to eat—poor tethered Dino. And afterwards with his horrid claws to kill, tear apart, anyone in the place, and eat all the human family. Its jaws, its appetites, were cruel.

The men now faced the forest, jumping and shouting. They wanted a sight of that horrible enemy before it was driven off. Boice-lat beat her drum.

Tirro made no attack. They heard it crashing its clumsy way into the distance. Scared off . . .

So then a celebration was held. They had scored a victory. They laughed and cheered. They drank mull, both males and females. Only when dawn peeped forth in the East, where the sea lay murmurously sleeping, did they fall or sprawl, to lie against one another, tired, totalled, and tossed into versions of sleep.

It had been a good night. Jork-flay rose and sang of it.

"We are the ones never to be eaten.
We dream and play, the very mountain-peak
Of humans who have learned to speak.
So sweet is life and we it sweeten!
Our cares we sling, we dare to sing—
The forest-monsters we have seized and beaten . . . "

And everyone joined in, women with their sweet voices. "The forest monsters we have seized and beaten."

It was the women, by and large, who cared for Dino, tethered in the swamp near which the river flowed to the sea. Dino was tame by now and ate what she was given. Some of the smaller boys were allowed to dare to sit on Dino's rubbery yellow hide.

The men, who called themselves warriors, did nothing. They lay about. Every so often the women forced them to go on a hunt. Then they would set off with spears and cudgels, whooping as they caught many small beasts, rats, deer, rabbits, foxes. Always looking out for the hulking carnivores that could spring on them.

This peaceful existence was broken into by the dreaded Tirro. The guard had fallen asleep on his platform. Tirro was charging furiously about the camp.

Two women were killed, including Kish-desh with her new baby. Forg it was who flung himself onto the monster's back, hacking at its throat until it fell dead.

Oh, and what a feast was held then! Under its armour Tirro's meat was exceptional tasty. For this, the brute had been born. They even threw a slice to Dino.

"How fortunate we are!" they all sang in chorus.

The Last of the Hound-Folk

There I stood, in one of the underground rooms of the Ashmolean Museum, lecturing about my writing and the relationship between time and imagining....

"My life," I said smugly to my audience, "resembles the shadowy meaning of one of my books. Not entirely comprehensible even to myself."

A fellow in the audience, sitting hunched up in a large overcoat, dark of face, black of hair, said, "I find your books entirely comprehensible, Angus—more's the pity. If you don't understand them, then surely you did not do your work thoroughly enough."

I was calm, even while finding myself vulnerable standing there. "The trouble is that I find I am stuck in the middle of the great silent wave of evolution. We have not yet grasped all the implications of evolution. Once there were early men without clothing, without art or industry. Now many of us—including you, sir, I assume, benefit from art and industry; perhaps we are subservient to those things... Yet one is aware that ahead of us—many generations ahead, perhaps terrifyingly far ahead, live people who will have developed capacities, with understandings we could not possibly understand."

A hush fell over the audience at my words. Someone giggled, quickly suppressing the sound.

As I stood there on the platform, there drifted—or clicked, rather—into my mind's eyes the figures in tombs of the Eighteenth Dynasty in Egypt, including those figures depicted in the tomb of Tutankamun. One in particular! That figure known as Anubis, a manlike figure with the head of a hound.

Anubis!

The name Anubis marks his importance as guardian of dead pharaohs and their tombs, associating him with processes of decline and death.

Anubis is clearly held with ancient Egyptian deities, Anubis assumes different roles in various contexts.

And as I stood transfixed, I saw—I realised—I understood—I was sure I understood—that there had once been a race of . . . well, of people, of hound-people. Hound-folk, dying out as the human race arrived on the scene. Anubis served among dead humanity—signifying—or so ran my tumultuous thoughts—that he was the last of his breed, this great Anubis with his black hound's body and skull.

Anubis! And as he stood for the extinction of his entire race, he also stood—could we but grasp the fact—for another great shift in the Earth's dominant populations, yes, for the far distant undeniable future eclipse of humanity, with all its brutality, its illusions, its unfathomable happinesses and sorrows.

And we would be superceded, much as hound-folk had been superceded in the days of ancient Egypt . . .

The audience, disconcerted by my silence, began to shuffle about. Some people were rising to their feet.

Mavis Hardcastle, the lady who had introduced me at the start of the evening, rose from her perch and thanked me warmly for my lecture. Clapping followed, scattered among the departing crowd.

"You all right, Angus?" she asked, searchingly.

"Oh, sorry, Mavis. I had a sudden revelation."

"How strange," she said, in guarded manner. "What was that about?"

"Oh, the distant future of humanity . . . Well, no, rather . . . " I was embarrassed; no one likes to appear silly, especially on a lecture platform. "Rather, the distant past, and someone, not a pharoah . . . ."

She was surveying me strangely. "So who . . . ?"

I said, "Let's go and have a drink, Mavis, and I'll tell you about it. It's Anubis, great Anubis . . . "

Munch

It was the year Strindberg died. Edvard Munch was in his garden. Here were apple trees, bearing their rosy fruit in the brief Nordic summer. Tall-stalked flowers stood about where the painter had not trampled them down. The distant fence was propped up with unpainted planks.

All this could be seen, or half-seen. Munch's left eye had burst and he feared oncoming blindness. He had executed paintings of the sun, the great golden sun, the blessed sun, father of us all. Always wished for. Sometimes actual.

He was well enough to paint. Jacobs, an enlightened nerve doctor, had diminished his alcoholism. He was now dealing with six large canvases, rapidly painted and slowly brought outside to be hung, to weather, to—in a word—to mature. Some paint would fall off when the frosts came.

Painting was all. His days bedazzled by the beauty of women's bodies were over, closed like a sacred book. Yet of a night he often remembered—what was her name? Was it Millie? A married woman, yet she had seduced him. They had laid together among tall silver trees. At one time they had fornicated where an ancient church stood, with pagan mounds nearby, as if equivalents of virtue and sin had been made for his contemplation.

And trees and sun—did they not prompt desire? Empty bottles lay in a ditch in long grass.

Oh yes, with Millie. Fickle and naughty Millie. What a bad world they lived in. Sex itself, its joyous relief that quickly fades, built up remorse in Munch's brain, with a pervasive melancholia. One is older now.

Well, well, painting remained. The painting of things extraordinary.

The sun bursting through the verticals of his copse. The dreamlife of the tubes of paint, squeezing their orgasms on to the palette. 'Foolish to think like that . . . '

What mattered was hanging these canvases to mature outside. They had to live.

In his late forties, alcoholism and depression had driven Munch to seek medical care. A Jewish doctor, Jacobs, had diagnosed dementia paralytica. Jacobs had walked with Munch through the city streets.

"The life of a man," Jacobs said, "is invariably improved by the works of others from earlier days—their thought processes."

And with a sly glance at his patient he added,

"At least you have the consolation of being a great artist, Edvard. That's better than any bottle of wine . . . Just remember that."

Munch did remember those words, and remembered them now as he endeavoured to hang his pictures like washing on the line. Was not being a great artist—an extra burden to drag through life? 'Even a mediocre artist', he told himself.

His troublesome thoughts wandered to his father, now dead. He recalled waiting for the Oslo coach. There stood his old dad, not waving, a bent old man in his best suit, in which to see his son away on a journey. Now he was himself old. 'The moving finger writes. And having writ, moves on . . . ' Some old poem, half-remembered.

At least some paintings would remain when he had gone. He rested his back against the wall of his house, to think again of August Strindberg. Did actors still perform 'The Ghost Sonata'? he wondered. Fashions came and went.

Much like people. Like famous authors, writing fantasy.

How little we would value the Sun if there was no such counterbalance as Night . . .

He lifted another canvas from the grass and pegged it to the line with the rough wooden pegs his old gardener had made. His gardener now working abroad.

What had that old feller said, "Some of these paintings aren't at all bad. You'll ruin them for sure, sticking them out here in the wind and the rain."

What had he said in reply? "They're mine, Jak. I can do what I like with them till I become too feeble to care."

"Keep such thoughts to yoursen," Jak retorted sharply.

Now, alone, Munch thought with a sigh that this was simply something he did. Pegging them out. Survive or die . . .

A woman's voice called from beyond the fence. He recognised her tone of voice. That would be Harriet, who, owing him money, came to cook a meal for him now and then.

"Edvard! Edvard!"

He did not answer. He dropped his canvas on the grass.

He stood against the wall of his house, hands behind his back. He felt the rough brick against his palms.

"Edvard! Will you neglect my care for you, damn you?!"

He made no reply.

Harriet rattled the gate. "Edvard, you famous feller!"

Still he made no reply.

The Music of Sound

This Sunday 4th April at 6 p.m., Darkis Zataviat will play Beethoven, Borodin, and Gravian pieces by Babian, Tawk Clunes & Nromia. Full details can be found on the website. A poster is attached.

Darkis Zataviat was struggling into his evening dress, assisted by his lover, Taylor May Tayler.

"Oh, I am furiously putting on weight," he said, indulgently chiding himself.

"Oh, you're not," said Taylor May. She had just dyed black her long mane of hair. "You don't eat enough. Far too many tangerines, not enough pasta . . . "

By way of response, he said, "I've only just discovered that Borodin was illegitimate. Fancy!"

"How did you find that out?"

"I read it in Gogol."

She gave a tiny chuckle. "Gogol says day-dreaming is a short-term detachment from one's immediate surroundings, Do you think that's so?"

"Could be that Borodin's mother had been recently widowed—say a week before he was born."

"What does it matter in any case?. . . Who do you think I met at the library this morning?"

He threw up a hand in mock-despair. "How should I know? A private detective."

"Indij Saxby. It must be eight years. We met her in Leningrad, remember? She was one of the English-speaking guides and we got chummy. Now she's married to an Englishman. Paul someone."

"St Petersberg. It's been rechristened. It's Leningrad no longer. Lenin's dead, old girl."

"She told me they have a daughter. They live in Stoney Stratford. What a name, eh? Stoney Stratford!"

"Borodin was a chemist. Did you know that? I wonder if he ever went on a trek to Central Asia. That must have been a wonderful thing to do in those days."

She surveyed herself in a mirror, saying thoughtfully,

"Someone was telling me that Benjamin Britten worked in the movies as a young man. Was it with T. S. Eliot? No . . . Possibly Auden?"

He was adjusting his bow tie.

"Y'know, I was reading somewhere about the various regions of the brain. It's still not properly understood, despite all the recent advances in neurology. There are sectors where apparently silence prevails, yet there must be something going on. It's uneasy-making to think that some kind of thought is in process of which we are unaware."

"Yes. Quite. Indij says they know a man with a brain injury after a bad road smash who provides clinically relevant information to doctors. Though he can't talk or anything. Doesn't that strike you as weird?"

"It's getting on for eight. Maybe we'd better be getting along now."

"They think he lit an electric light the other day, just by thought projection. There was an account of it in 'The Independent' last week."

"I haven't seen a copy of 'The Independent' for ages . . . "

Taylor May was checking her lipstick in the hall mirror.

"I must get to Barclay's tomorrow," she said.

"I'll take you there," Darkis said.

They went out into the night, where their car and chauffeur were awaiting them.

"I must see the supervisor. It's a woman, thank god."

"1880 . . . Central Asia . . . must have been rather more central in Borodin's day."

The cab was taking them to the concert hall in good time.

Taylor May Tayler went on talking.

Zataviat held her hand.

He was humming to himself, while wondering where in the brain music originated. And talk, come to that . . .

The Silent Cosmos

It was Sacred Day 35 by our reckoning and I was so proud. To me was awarded an Aspects of Resistance, Second Grade, by the Master Insuffaller himself. I swore to deny the Western Scientific Approach and went down on my knees, where my forehead touched the stone floor.

This ceremony took place in the Atrium of Telepanthic Abilities. Only my especial friend, Mouwse was allowed as witness. But throughout the Interstices, our great flock was also feeding on the ceremony.

Afterwards, afterwards came music, The Drag, and pulse to drink. For the first time in my True Life, I was spoken to with real lips by the celebrated Consecrator. I banished prudence from my character outline and conversed with him in real empathy.

"I forsee the time is coming when the universe will reach a favourable stage of evolution," I said.

In full accord, he answered, "Our universe is not as
Outsiders view it, not a jot.
They are blind, with eyes like metal.
Their universe is sterile—they would kill us all alive.
Our universe is like a honey pot,
Full of flying intelligences much like bees in a hive."

Thus this great man summed up in poetry our main beliefs.

Certainly our beliefs and understandings had brought us under threat. Forced our Removal to this dull site in the Cosmos.

For Belief's reason, we had freed ourselves from Western Scientific Approach. Our earthly planetoid was set far into the wilds of Grand Siberia, on an upper paleolithic plain. We knew this place as Kanstantin. From Kanstantin we could affirm we were in touch telepathically with a variety of other beings elsewhere, many dark years distant.

We were forbidden to touch anyone below the belt. My friend Mouwse and I tapped each other on the chest before we went to sleep. We slept in rows on the floor. Our experts had invented and provided traumasnoo. With traumasnoo we did not dream at all. The rumour ran that the outside world had invented a dream-seeker, whereby they could read dreams—our dreams—from a distance, and so learn our secrets from us. Traumasnoo had come along just in time, as is the way with providence. I felt its dull throb in my skull of a night.

So we slept and were unconscious while the mighty Cosmos wheeled about us. One day, it was promised, they would come for us and take us—take us to where there was no metal or machinery. No vegetation. I awoke, knowing I was now an Aspect of Resistance. Mouwse tapped my chest and I his—Mouwse's pretty little chest, without hair.

Following Ceremony Day there were no set Communications. I drank my Pulse-plus and then went out. Compelled to breathe.

I walked, legs instructed, by the roaring river. Its banks were crusted by ice. Small trees were still bare of leaves. Verily, this was a cosmic aspect. Nevertheless, I could not understand why I suddenly felt myself to be in misery, of misery. Had I sinned?

When I steadied myself against a sapling and looked up to the sky, I saw nothing beyond the clouded air rushing above me.

A great terror seized me. I was asking was there nothing beyond. Only silence . . . What if this sacred place of ours stood alone in a cosmic silence, and there was nothing, no one, in all the vast rotating universe?

The terrible prospect of an enclosing solitude stripped me mentally naked. In that exterior world, the world of 'science' from which we of Telepathic Abilities had been forced to hide—there was not one person in a million who concerned him or herself about communication with the vast Cosmos.

Could it possibly be that they were right and we wrong? . . .

The sapling on which I depended bent and snapped. I slithered down the small bank, and one boot entered icy water.

What could that signify? A cosmos of ice and flame only?

I called to the Consecrator for reasurance but no answer came. I looked about me. Only the dreadful neutral wilderness of nature greeted my gaze.

I asked myself, *What is intelligence? Where has it led me?*

Weeping, I began to walk, following the rushing waters.

There had to be something, I told myself, something we could never know, even among the learned of us—about the great Cosmos—about our little selves . . .

Writings on the Rock

Further to my recent May report on the ongoing Gizini excavations near Antofagasta. Antofagasta is situated on the West coast of Chile, almost on the Tropic of Capricorn. It is reckoned to have been the centre of Gizinian culture, nine centuries B.C., and long since utterly destroyed.

Researches on this site and a neighbouring one have continued for over six years, under the patronage of South America Science Institutions Inc.

On a day in 1939, I had a visitor to our little centre, tucked up in the mountains, high above Antofagasta, above the shining sea. This man had been a famous film actor in France, Torrance de Tamsin. His brother-in-law, Jimmy Bale was head of the team working to interpret the Gizini heiroglyphs.

Bale was explaining one of their problems.

"This lump of rock, Rock No.127 from Store 2, was believed to be minutely decorated. These markings I find to be a form of early script, passages of which I have deciphered."

He grinned. "Remember the Rosetta Stone?"

He ran over a preliminary report. "But some items still baffle us, are not yet properly understood. A word for instance not yet properly translatable."

"Such as?" de Tamsin asked, pretending to care.

"Well, this word here." Bale indicated a stone symbol with his thumb nail. "It really has to be the Gizinian term for *'animals'*, but in context it's baffling."

He gave his brother-in-law the script of a passage he had translated and printed out.

The Gizinian read, "We rejoice ourselves! We know that the *'animals'* lead us. They are free of *temperament* or temperaments. We are prisoners of our temperaments. This is what *'disallows'* us. We tell of ourselves that we can swing at any time to turn *happy* or *sad*. There come depressions. So we are governed by emotions, rather than being *calm*, and do not behave with the balance that the *'animals'* above us use. All of 'philosophy' must work upon these principles.

"We realise that when 'God' brought life to this world, he did not see humans, *who were hidden*? And so balance was not given to our frames as to those 'on whom we depend'.

"So it shows because we are servants of those forever calm and enduring that our culture will last for ever by the shining sea."

"Such texts have yet to be understood," Bale admitted.

The Light Really

It was the light really. I had broken my leg. It was all bandaged up and I was not checking in to the paper for a day or two. The summer sunshine was so pleasant that I just opted for lounging about.

Besides, I was getting over that long interview with the man known as P. M. Muluzi.

So I was just sitting about in my flat. Totally alone, of course. My wife, Doreen, Dainty Doreen, had left me, citing my affairs with other women. I really couldn't blame her. She was quite decent about it.

She phoned me now and then. She was living with her mum in Bridlington, on the coast, or so she said.

The leg was a touch tedious. A nurse, pretty, coloured, possibly twenty-five, came in every morning to attend to it. I thought about her in a predatory way, but had yet to strike.

So by and large there was little for me to do—apart from that interview with Mr. P. M. I sat around in shafts of light, reading quite a bit. Some interesting books from Doreen's day—nothing about Malawi, P. M.'s Malawi, of course—but for instance an illustrated book on the art of Bill Viola. She'd liked Viola, but I couldn't properly understand what he was all about.

So mainly I sat around in different rooms, according to the light, sometimes reading, sometimes not.

This is a small house, but good on windows. As the day creeps by, the light changes: brightness here, slumberous quality there.

I went a bit poetical. The extraordinary gift of sunlight gets distributed throughout the day—early on, dazzling in the kitchen, towards evening browsing in my tiny front room where—having emailed on my piece to the paper—I sit to write this kind of stuff.

Now it's mid-day. Or more like one o'clock. I listen to the BBC's latest depressing news about the recession. I am limping about the house and the strip of garden, gathering up stuff for my lunch. In a little glass extension on the kitchen some washing hangs. The rays of the sun pour in, narrowly avoiding the roof of the house next door, where Logan and Daisy, his missus, live.

For contrast, my gas cooker stands in shadow, looking dark and broody. Maybe like me it's sick of work. Anyhow, I light a burner. So I'm preparing things for my lunch. It was Doreen's recipe—Doreen had lived with a Russian chap on the paper before we met up. She had been utterly chaste, so she claimed. Of course . . .

The phone rang. Doreen.

"It's Doreen, Jack. Hi! Just wondering how you were."

"Just about to enjoy lunch."

"Have you got a nice pork pie, Jack?"

"'An Eagle Never Sings'. Mean anything to you?"

"Oh yes, lovely song, isn't it! Do you like it?"

"Well, I'm busy just now, old girl."

"Are you happy, Jack?"

Sigh. "Aren't you happy? Enjoying the seaside? You recall we separated?"

"Oh, I don't really know if I'm ever truly happy. Something in my disposition . . . Do you understand what I'm really saying, Jack?"

"Sorry dear, the saucepan's boiling. Must go. You remember you left me, don't you?"

"Don't say that, please. You hurt me, Jack. I was thinking—"

"Darling, we've split. There's no going back. Besides, my borscht is calling me."

"I just rang to see if you were okay, darling."

The borscht was ready.

I'd soon find another woman. There was that dark-haired Jean, one of the reporters on *The Guardian* . . .

I carried the saucepan and a soup spoon into the sun filtering into my little two-chairs-and-a-sofa living room, settled myself with the saucepan on my lap and steadily enjoyed my lunch.

Later, when sunshine was flowing in the rear window, I got down to work. I had till six o'clock to get my piece in to *The Guardian*.

On the previous day, I had interviewed Petir Mandor Muluzi, or "P. M. Muluzi", a celebrity from Malawi, a large and handsome black man currently singing his own songs on a London stage. ("An Eagle Never Sings" becoming a hit.) He had also published a novel, selling well, about three people moving from Malawi to Europe and back. His was a remarkable success, emerging from a relatively obscure country.

He was swollen with his success, and boastful about it. While listening to P.M. talking, I took a dislike to him, and to his frequent references to Karl Marx. All the same, the paper wanted a success story. So that was what I sent them.

Maybe, I thought, I had been jealous of Muluzi's success. But all would fade away in another month and he would retire to the heat and obscurity of his Malawi . . . and the world would forget him . . .

Why had I done nothing of that sort? I was just a by-line on a daily paper. As daylight faded on the day, I suddenly decided I would sleep out in my garden—as I had once done with Doreen.

That would show them!

Summer day was passing into summer night when I lugged a couple of blankets, pillow and torch into a patch of grass by the west wall. I kept my clothes on and made myself as comfortable as possible. With the light and the warmth, feeling myself coddled, I drifted off into the mystery zone of dreams.

Darkness enfolded me and everything else.

What woke me was a woman's voice raised in anger.

"No! No, Harry, let go of me. They're bound to see us!"

I couldn't hear his response. They were talking from the next garden, on the other side of the wall. "Stop it, Harry—or I'll yell for Logan!"

I visualised the scene. Two couples, Harry and Daisy—I was sure I recognised Daisy's voice—Daisy and Logan lived next door, and so Logan was in the house with Harry's—whoever Harry was—with Harry's wife.

Daisy was shouting at this Harry a bit now. Suddenly I thought, 'My god, if he jumps over the wall, he'll land on me . . . '

Not a week ago, I had had to jump over a wall to escape an angry husband. Unfortunately, there had been an elaborate concrete bird bath on the other side, where I landed. That was where I broke my leg.

So now I rose from my blankets rather hastily and shouted over the wall. "Let her alone, Harry, you dirty blighter!"

He rushed to the wall and peered angrily over. "Who the hell do you think you are? Mind your own bloody business!"

Switching on my torch, I flashed it into his big red face.

"I'm the parish priest, sir," I told him.

He disappeared. I heard her laugh contemptuously as they made their way back into Daisy's house.

I had won that round! Perhaps it was my pretence of being a priest that had done it. But to my mind it was the light really.

The Mistake They Made

Madagascar was always a unique place. The island had drifted away from the sub-continent of India many millennia ago. And I was the man who discovered that that drifting was no mere geological accident.

A seismic fault had been discovered along the East coast of India. And discovered by whom? By the Dnogkikkin to use the label by which they call themselves.

Long ago, in the mists of time and geology, more than one kind of humanic race inhabited the globe. Apart from humanity and Neanderthal and the Leopard people, there were also the Dnogkikkin.

As I stood close to the summit of Antsirana, gazing north over the Indian Ocean, I thought of those amazing Dnogkikkins, who had developed a particular state of mind which they called—I had read and translated their hieroglyphs on pottery 'volumes'—*'the knowing and feeling life-bond'.*

My name is Gussy Tom Fielding C.B.E.. I worked until recently in the P&GC, the Planning and Governmental Commission, of the state of Andhra Pradesh. This populous state, forever in a kind of uproar, is situated on the East coast of India. It was from Pradesh, in the main, that Madagascar had been torn. Geology was my intense hobby, and my holiday occupation with my wife, Ojal.

In a cupboard in the rear of an old shop in the present day capital, Antananarivo, we found old documents relating to the division of Madagascar from the Indian continent, that event taking place some 88 million years ago.

There were, of course, no written records dating from that distant age; only a yellowed leg bone or two survived the centuries. But antequarians existed, the hunters of their day. Ojal, conversing for over a year with learned ancients on Madagascar, gradually gained details of items that could be constructed into what seemed a convincing legend of the long-expired past.

Those ancient Dnogkikkin folk had always been in quest of an undeniable wisdom and the peace brought about by wisdom. They had seen to it, for instance that when their lands became that great island, the fourth largest in the world, free of continental violence, no monkeys or apes—those mischief-makers from which humanity was to descend were allowed. Lemurs, yes, they passed muster, and the harmless lemur evolved into many differing tribes over the ages, without giving offence. And the yak. Ah, the yak . . .

Yes, the yak, *bos mutus*, as we know it today. A gentle quadruped, shaggy of flank, wide of forehead. And not hostile towards the Dnogkikkins. Something of an alliance—so Ojal was told over many smoking pipes—was forged between yak and native. So much so that gradually no animal was killed for meat. With vegetarianism went a love for fish and shellfish, such as crab. And they cultivated a semi-aquatic paddy.

There in that sleepy tropical climate—or even when their world was lashed by tropical monsoons—man and quadruped developed a dominant creed, '*the knowing and feeling life-bond*'. This rapturous teaching was, so my dear wife discovered, developed with *feeling* from the yak and knowing from the tribe. (One has to use these words, but there is no precise translation of them from the language of the Dnogkikkin tongue.) We could learn the words of their songs, but not their music.

I am retired now. We—this old pair of us from the world's distinct parts!—we wrote and published our account of what we had built together: numberless centuries of that remarkable life-bond between a form of mankind and an animal. Our book appeared from the learned press of an American university, and only later, with abridgements, from a publisher in Germany.

And what, you may ask, happened to these mild, happy, bronze-skinned men and women of the Dnogkikkin race, together with their affectionate shaggy allies?

Long lazy centuries passed. Until men in boats, men in sailing ships, members of the Human race, brave predatory men, ambitious all, came to call in Madagascan ports. The pacific beings there, people of a sweet vulnerable kind, they and their mild and shaggy allies, welcomed these newcomers.

That was the mistake they made.

Brian Aldiss was born in Norfolk in 1925. After leaving the army, Brian worked as a bookseller, providing the setting for his first book, *The Brightfount Diaries* (1955). His first published science fiction work was the story 'Criminal Record', which appeared in *Science Fantasy* in 1954. Since then he has written over 300 short stories and nearly 100 books, including the acclaimed novels *Hothouse, Non-stop* and the *Helli-conia* series, all regarded as modern classics. In 2010 *The Hand-Reared-Boy* (1970) was longlisted for the Lost Booker Prize. His most recent SF novel is *Finches of Mars*.

Several of Brian's books, inc-luding *Frankenstein Unbound*, have been adapted for the cinema and his story 'Supertoys Last All Summer Long' was adapted and released as the film *AI* in 2001. Besides his own writing, Brian has edited numerous anthologies of science fiction and fantasy stories and the magazine *SF Horizons*.

Brian is a vice-president of the international H. G. Wells Soc-iety and in 2000 was given the Damon Knight Memorial Grand Master Award by the Science Fiction Writers of America. In 2005 he was awarded the OBE for services to literature. He lives in Oxford, where his bookselling career began in 1947.